ALMOST PERFECT

Also by Maggie Dana

Keeping Secrets, Timber Ridge Riders (Book 1)
Racing into Trouble, Timber Ridge Riders (Book 2)
Riding for the Stars, Timber Ridge Riders (Book 3)
Wish Upon a Horse, Timber Ridge Riders (Book 4)
Chasing Dreams, Timber Ridge Riders (Book 5)

The Golden Horse of Willow Farm, Weekly Reader Books
Remember the Moonlight, Weekly Reader Books
Best Friends series, Troll Books

TIMBER RIDGE RIDERS

Book Six

ALMOST PERFECT

Maggie Dana

PAGEWORKS PRESS

#6

ISBN 978-0-9851504-5-7

Edited by Judith Cardanha
Cover by Margaret Sunter
Interior design by Anne Honeywood
Published by Pageworks Press
Text set in Sabon

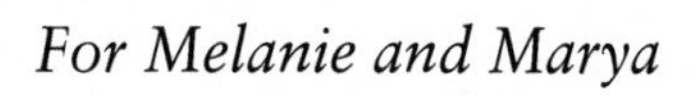

For Melanie and Marya

1

KATE MCGREGOR'S CELL PHONE buzzed while she was brushing her horse. Tapestry snorted and skittered sideways, ears on full alert as if she were afraid.

"Silly girl," Kate whispered.

She pulled out her phone, checked caller ID, and sighed. This was Adam's third call since lunch. His last one had caught her on the school bus and she'd had to pretend it was a wrong number.

"Hi," Adam said. "Can you talk?"

Kate shot a quick look at her best friend, Holly Chapman, grooming Magician in the next stall. Holly's face was smeared with dirt and her blond ponytail swung back and forth as she curried her black gelding's hindquarters. He'd been rolling in the mud again.

Lowering her voice, Kate said, "What's up?"

"Change of plans," Adam yelled above the noise of horses clattering by. He was obviously at Larchwood, the barn where he rode. "We can't—"

"Hold on," Kate said while Adam was still talking. She stuffed the phone in her pocket, slipped out of Tapestry's stall, and shut herself in the tack room. No way did she want Holly to overhear this conversation. She was already suspicious enough.

Kate retrieved her phone. "Can't what?"

"We can't have Holly's party at Brad's house."

"Why not?" Nervously, Kate tucked a strand of brown hair behind one ear and glanced at the door. If Holly barged in, she'd have to hang up.

"Big group of skiers coming in for the weekend," Adam said. "They're taking the whole place over, so there's no room for us."

Brad Piretti's parents owned the Timber Ridge ski resort. Their lodge was perfect for parties, and they'd offered to host Holly's surprise party on Saturday night. The whole thing was Adam's idea, and he'd even come up with the perfect theme—a *Holly*wood party for Holly because she loved glamour and old movies.

But without a place to hold it, they were sunk. Holly's house was too small, and Kate's was even smaller. Besides, she and her father had only just moved in and had barely begun to unpack. They'd been eating off paper plates and tripping over boxes for the past five days.

"Now what?" Kate said, feeling close to panic.

"The Timber Ridge clubhouse," Adam said. "Mr. Piretti's arranged for us to have Holly's party there instead."

"Awesome," Kate said. "That's even better than the lodge."

The clubhouse had an indoor pool, a gigantic hot tub, and a sound system that rocked. Kate made a mental note to tell everyone to bring bathing suits. Then reality kicked in and she groaned. The clubhouse was next door to Angela Dean's house, which meant that she and her bratty cousin would be able to gatecrash—just the very thing they'd worked hard to avoid. Holly would have a serious meltdown if Angela and Courtney showed up, uninvited, at her birthday party.

Correction. They'd *all* have a meltdown.

"I'll e-mail everyone," Adam said, and hung up as the tack room door swung open.

"Nathan?" Holly said, nodding at Kate's phone.

Kate hesitated. "Um, no."

Nathan was her boyfriend—well, sort of—but he was shooting a film in New Zealand and rarely had a chance to call. They'd met that summer when part of the *Moonlight* movie was shot at Timber Ridge and

Kate had ridden as a stunt double for Nathan's co-star, Tess O'Donnell.

Holly gave a snort of impatience. "Okay, then don't tell me."

Behind her came the other riding team members, followed by Liz Chapman, Holly's mom, who ran the stables.

"Hurry up, girls," Liz said. "Lesson in five minutes."

They were practicing for the next big event—an indoor horse show at Fox Meadow Hunt Club in mid-December. Only three girls would make the riding team, and Kate was determined to be one of them.

She grabbed her saddle, plucked Tapestry's bridle off its peg, and avoided Holly's piercing blue eyes as she left the tack room. By tomorrow night, all this subterfuge would be over, and she could stop pretending she wasn't talking to Holly's boyfriend when she clearly was. They'd been texting and calling each other for three weeks, swapping ideas and making plans. The other day Holly had gotten so ticked off about Kate's mysterious phone calls, she'd accused her of crushing on Adam.

It had taken all of Kate's willpower *not* to spill the beans.

* * *

Inside the Timber Ridge arena, Jennifer West took the lead on her chestnut gelding, Rebel. Close behind came Sue Piretti riding Tara, her sturdy Appaloosa, followed by Robin Shapiro on Chantilly, a dapple gray mare whose dished face and small ears hinted at Arabian blood, and Holly on Magician.

Bringing up the rear on Tapestry, Kate watched the stiff set of Holly's shoulders. She'd never seen Holly so tense, not even when she first began riding again after her accident.

"Don't crowd one another," Liz called from the middle of the ring. "Spread out. There's plenty of room."

Holly reined in Magician and looked back at Kate, but she didn't smile. There was no sign of Angela, the team's sixth member. She rarely showed up for riding practice and only rode when there was an appreciative audience. Her bay gelding, Skywalker, whinnied anxiously from the barn, as if he hated being left out.

Kate knew exactly how he felt.

This surprise party was wrecking her friendship with Holly. They'd spent the whole summer living together at Holly's house while Kate's dad was in Brazil researching rare butterflies, and they'd become the best friends ever. They shared absolutely everything—until Adam started calling Kate five times a day to talk about the party. Holly knew something was up and suspected the worst—that Kate was trying to take Adam away from her, which was totally crazy. Adam Randolph was like the older brother Kate always wanted but never had.

"Okay, girls," Liz said. "Let's have a nice flat-footed walk."

The lesson sped by. They circled at the trot and canter, took turns going over the jump course, and listened intently while Liz dished out equal amounts of criticism and praise. After a half hour, Kate forgot about the awkwardness between her and Holly and lost herself in the joy of riding her very own horse.

She'd only owned Tapestry since midsummer, but already she couldn't imagine life without her—pretty much the way she felt about Holly. They'd liked each other from the start when Kate had taken the job as a summer companion to Holly who had been confined to wheelchair after a car accident.

So much had happened since then that Kate could hardly believe it. Holly had learned to walk and ride again, they'd competed together for the riding team, and Kate's biggest dream had come true—her father had sold their condo in Connecticut and moved to Winfield, Vermont. He'd become the director of Dancing Wings, the largest butterfly museum in New England. Kate often felt like dancing herself as she rode her bike to the barn after school, and—

"Kate, wake up," Liz said. "You're on the wrong diagonal."

Blushing, Kate sat for two beats and corrected herself.

* * *

As they left the arena, Holly rode alongside Kate. She shrugged and said, "You wanna, like, hang out tonight?"

"I can't," Kate blurted. "I promised to help Dad."

Boy, did that sound totally lame. But it was the first thing that popped into her head. In reality, she was going straight to Jennifer's house with Robin and Sue to finish making party decorations. Then they were going to the clubhouse to scope out the room Mr. Piretti had reserved. Adam was supposed to meet them there.

"Whatever," Holly said with a scowl.

Knowing she'd just made a bad situation even worse, Kate led Tapestry into her stall. She should've ditched the decorating session and let the others handle it. Besides, she wasn't much good with glue and scissors and would probably make a big mess anyway.

But . . . too late now.

Without another word, Holly yanked off Magician's tack. She dumped it on the ground and rubbed her horse down with angry, jerky movements. When she got like this, Kate knew it was best to keep her distance. They'd only had one other fight, and it was Adam who'd talked Kate into calling Holly to apologize. But now his plans for a surprise party had landed Kate on Holly's hit list.

Feeling glum, Kate brushed her mare's copper-colored coat and finger-combed the knots from her flaxen mane and tail. For once, Tapestry's stunning good looks failed to cheer her up.

* * *

"C'mon, Kate," Jennifer said, waving a glue gun. "Holly doesn't think you're trying to steal Adam."

"Yes, she does," Kate muttered.

"That's crazy," Sue said. "You're her best friend."

"I know," Kate said. "But right now she's treating me like her worst enemy."

"She's just suspicious, that's all," Robin said.

"So why does she think I'm trying to swipe her boyfriend instead of the obvious, like we just might be planning a surprise party?" Kate said. "I mean, Holly's not stupid, she's—"

"Feeling left out?" Robin said.

"Yeah," Kate said. "And I worry about it."

Sue gave a gasp. "You're not gonna *tell* her, are you?"

"No," Kate said, but she wanted to.

Bits of glitter stuck to her hands. She tried to wipe them off and got silvery stuff all over her hoodie. Sighing, she put down the star she'd just cut out. Its edges were all jaggy, not smooth and slick like the ones Robin and Sue were creating at dizzying speed.

Jennifer's kitchen was awash with curly pink ribbons and silver glitter that got in everyone's hair, up their noses, and all over the counters. Jen's mother laughed it off and continued pulling delicious looking chocolate cupcakes from her oven. Tomorrow, she told the girls, she would make mini quiches and a vegetable platter with three dips. All the riding team parents were pitching in to help—except for Mrs. Dean, of course.

Kate worried about that as well.

Maybe they should've invited Angela and Courtney, just to be on the safe side. The others told her she was nuts. But Kate had a horrible suspicion that Angela and her cousin would find a way to trash Holly's surprise party.

* * *

The Timber Ridge party room had sliding glass doors that opened onto the indoor pool. Along its far wall stood fake palms and striped umbrellas with bistro tables and chairs. There was even a long red carpet for the guests to walk on, just like at a movie premiere or the Oscars.

"I bet someone falls into the hot tub," Robin said, eyeing it carefully.

"Yeah, like a *real* Hollywood party!" said Sue.

Kate glanced at the disco ball, spinning overhead. Amid colored spotlights, it splintered the pool's surface into a million fragments. Holly was going to love this. She swam like a dolphin, so Kate made a mental note to e-mail Liz and remind her to bring Holly's bathing suit tomorrow night.

Holly's actual birthday wasn't until Sunday, but the plan was for Liz to take Holly and Adam out for a fancy dinner on Saturday night. That way, Holly would be all dressed up with makeup and everything. But before going to the restaurant, they would stop at the clubhouse to pick up some paperwork Liz needed. She'd send Holly inside to get it, and that's when they'd all jump out and yell, "Surprise!"

Adam emerged from the sound booth where he'd

been setting up the party music—a mix of the latest hits and songs from Holly's favorite musicals. "I've just had another great idea," he said.

"What?" Kate said.

So far, his ideas had been awesome. He'd gotten ahold of movie posters—*Grease*, *Mary Poppins*, and *Flashdance*—to hang on the walls and even managed to borrow an old-fashioned popcorn machine that actually worked.

"I'm gonna cancel my date with Holly," Adam said, pulling out his cell phone. "It'll really throw her a curve. She'll never guess we're throwing her a surprise party instead."

"No way," Kate yelled. "Don't you dare!"

Jennifer sighed. "Bad move, dude."

But Adam ignored them, and Kate watched in horror as his thumbs flew over the keypad. Poor Holly. She'd be devastated and there was nothing Kate could do about it.

"She'll be cool with it," he said. "Don't panic."

"You'd better be right," Kate said. She was tempted to push him into the hot tub. "Or I'll never talk to you again."

"Speaking of panic," Sue said, "I've got nothing to wear."

Neither did Kate. She didn't even own a dress, never

mind a long gown. The only time she'd gotten dressed up, like *really* dressed up, was when she wore a floaty white dress for her stunt-double role in *Moonlight.*

"So, who's got a Lady Gaga castoff hanging in *her* closet?" Robin said, sounding morose.

"Not me," Sue replied. "The only castoffs I've got are my sister's, and she's got the fashion sense of a hippie."

Jennifer laughed. "No problem."

They would hit the Salvation Army thrift shop first thing the next morning, where, she promised, they would find the dress of their dreams for less than fifteen dollars.

"Cheap and sparkly," she said. "With lots of bling."

"Totally glam," Robin added.

Sue tossed her head. "I want sequins, a feather boa, and high heeled boots."

"You can't," Adam said, pretending to pout.

"Why not?"

"Because that's what *I'm* wearing."

Jennifer shoved Adam so hard, he almost fell into the hot tub.

2

THE THRIFT SHOP WAS FAR from glamorous, but Jen was right about the amazing selection of clothes. It had racks and racks of evening gowns, prom dresses, and bridesmaids' outfits in every size and color. Kate felt as if she were rummaging through a bag of giant lollipops.

"How's this for ten bucks?" Sue said, holding up an orange cocktail dress dripping with feathers.

"Great, if you're a chicken," Robin said.

Kate pulled a sparkly gold dress off the rack and hugged it to herself. "What do you think?"

"That looks like a jar of mustard," Jennifer said, shaking her head. She handed Kate a long silky dress that matched her green eyes. "Try this. It's totally cool."

Moments later, Kate couldn't believe it when she

saw herself in the full-length mirror. The dress shimmered as she twirled around, and a cloud of blue-green chiffon cascaded from her shoulders like the fins of an exotic fish. It had skinny straps and a skinny tie belt with silver tassels on the ends.

"Perfect," Jennifer declared.

Kicking off her sneakers, Robin tried on a puffy red dress with a sequined top and multiple layers, and Sue had them in fits of giggles when she clumped out of the fitting room in her paddock boots and a frothy white crinoline that reminded Kate of a wedding cake.

"Cinderella rides again," Kate said.

Then Jennifer stole the show by tottering past on four-inch heels, wearing elbow-length black gloves and a strapless blue gown with a bias-cut skirt that flared from her knees like a wave. Over one arm, she carried a beaded purse. Peeking out the top was a tiny stuffed poodle.

Hands on both hips, Sue struck a pose. "Fah-bulous, dah-link."

"What about Holly?" Kate said, folding up her new dress. "She won't be wearing something like this. She's gonna feel awful."

"So, we'll get her a dress, too," Robin said.

"The glitzier the better," Sue added.

Dresses, skirts, and tops flew about as they pawed

through the racks again. Finally, they settled on a purple satin dress with silver straps and a ruffled hem. Jennifer completed the outfit by producing a long silver cape trimmed with fake ermine that she found in a dress-up box.

"Ta-dah!" she said. "We can throw this around her when she walks in. Then she can change into her dress after all the fuss is over."

Kate plucked a tiara off a shelf.

"Princess Holly," Robin said.

After trying on shoes, they picked out the biggest pair of sunglasses they could find and stood in line at the checkout counter. Jennifer pulled three feather boas off a hook and wound them around her neck.

"For Adam," she said.

* * *

Holly stepped out of the shower, wrapped herself in a towel, and rubbed steam off the bathroom mirror. Tomorrow, she would turn fifteen. Would she look any different than she did now? More grown-up, a whole year older? Would she feel, somehow, a little bit smarter? She put a hand to her face. Maybe her zits would vanish and she'd finally be able to understand linear equations, thanks to the magic of just one more day.

But she'd heard that going from fourteen to fifteen was no big deal, not like reaching sixteen when you could get a job and a driver's license. Now *that* was totally cool. Besides, you got to have a Sweet Sixteen party with all the bells and whistles. And that's exactly what Holly wanted.

Well, why not a Fabulous Fifteen party?

But none of her friends had said one word about tomorrow—not even Kate, and Holly knew her the best. She'd been keeping her eyes and ears open, hoping for a clue, something that would tell her people really did know, or even care, it was her birthday.

Everyone was blowing her off.

They'd been avoiding her like she smelled bad or had sprouted an extra ear. First, Kate was always too busy helping her dad unpack, and then Adam had totally finked out.

Holly still couldn't believe it.

She grabbed her cell phone and shook it, like it was the phone's fault she hadn't heard from Adam since last night when he canceled their date. His mom had a babysitting crisis, and he had to stay home and take care of his little brother.

C U on Sunday instead? he'd texted.

Forget it, Holly had texted back.

Rewrapping her towel, Holly flopped onto her unmade bed. Mom had said to get dressed up, but for once, Holly didn't feel like it. She didn't even want to bother with make-up and fixing her hair. Who cared, anyway? It was just the two of them going to a stupid French restaurant in the village when all Holly wanted was a pizza with her friends.

She stared at Kate's empty bed.

She'd only been gone for five days, but already it felt like five years. A tear rolled down Holly's cheek. Angrily, she wiped it away. She would *not* cry over this. It wasn't the end of the world because her best friend was trying to steal her boyfriend and nobody was paying the slightest attention to her birthday.

Well, except for Mom.

There was a soft knock on the door. "You ready yet?"

"I don't wanna go," Holly said, snuggling beneath her pony print comforter. Books and magazines tumbled off the bed. She reached down and plucked her latest *Moonlight* from the floor, replaced the bookmark, and stuck it on her night table. On the back cover was a photo of Tess O'Donnell and Nathan Crane—Kate's boyfriend—but the tabloids and gossip mags hadn't caught on yet. The studio had kept really quiet about Nathan's relationship with Holly's best friend.

Some best friend she'd turned out to be.

* * *

Kate stared with dismay at the make-up Jennifer had helped her buy at the drugstore—blush, eye shadow, mascara, and a jar of something called "concealer." What was it supposed to conceal? Her nose? Eyebrows? That stupid spot that had erupted on her chin this morning? Holly was the expert at all this, not her. Kate didn't know one end of a lipstick from the other, but she'd have to find out in a hurry because there was nobody to help.

Her father poked his head around the door. Spatters of white had turned his hair and beard from brown to grizzled. He'd been painting the kitchen and from the looks of things, getting more paint on himself than on the walls. "How are you doing?"

"Don't ask," Kate said.

He held out a paintbrush. "Would this help?"

Kate threw a cotton ball at him.

Laughing, he disappeared. It was odd seeing him like this, doing ordinary stuff that ordinary fathers did. He'd spent most of Kate's life traipsing through jungles from Borneo to Brazil in search of rare butterflies.

Ever since Kate's mom died five years ago, he'd hardly been home at all, and Kate had been passed from one elderly relative to another like a dusty heir-loom nobody was quite sure what to do with. But now, finally, they were learning to be a family, thanks to Aunt Marion who'd loaned them her cottage for the winter. Next spring, they'd have to find somewhere else to live. There was a house for sale at Timber Ridge. It sat across from Angela Dean's house and was kind of expensive, but—

No, not a good idea.

Kate glanced at her bed, covered with Holly's spare pony print sheets and comforter. She'd insisted that Kate take them with her when she moved out of the Chapmans' house a week ago.

"It'll make us feel more connected," Holly had said. She'd also given Kate her favorite stuffed animal—a black-and-white pony that reminded her of Adam's horse, Domino. "Just for a little while until you, like, settle in," she'd said. "Then you can give him back."

Would Holly want him back now?

Kate picked up the soft little pinto, gave him a hug, and tucked him into the bag that held her gift for Holly—leather riding gloves and a pink t-shirt that said *Best Friends Ride Forever*.

Gritting her teeth, Kate tackled the make-up. She

dabbed and smeared, then wiped it all off and started again. If she could jump her horse over a four-foot fence, surely she could figure out how to stick a little glitter on her eyelids without making a monumental mess.

* * *

The party room twinkled with fairy lights, silver stars, and sparkly streamers. Adam had hung his movie posters on the walls and Brad Piretti, who was so tall he didn't need a ladder, was tying bunches of hot pink balloons to light fixtures and curtain rods. Both boys wore dark pants, dress shirts, and bow ties. Adam had gone one step further and borrowed his father's tux. His jacket lay slung over a chair. Tucked inside one pocket, Kate could see a tiny gold box. Holly's gift?

More gifts were stacked on a table—a pile of bags and boxes tied with huge bows and colorful ribbons. Kate added her gift and tried not to feel self-conscious. She'd worn jeans and breeches for so long, she'd forgotten how it felt to wear a dress. Was her makeup okay? Had she used too much? Not enough? What about her hair? She'd left it loose, tucked behind one ear. Holly had once told she looked like Emma Watson that way.

"It's perfect," Jennifer said.

She'd ramped up her outfit with a long string of pearls and earrings the size of small spoons. Her auburn hair fell in a wedge over one eye like a 1920s flapper, and Kate had no clue how her friend managed to stagger about in those outrageous shoes.

A man wearing dark glasses and three cameras slung around his neck walked by. He wore a black hat with a card tucked in its brim that said "Press."

"Who's that?" Kate said.

Jennifer grinned. "My dad. He's pretending to be one of those awful paparazzi."

Then Sue and Robin ran over, and Kate gasped. Robin's brown curls tumbled in soft ringlets around her face, and someone had braided tiny pink roses into Sue's sandy red hair. Their eyes sparkled, their cheeks glowed, and they looked nothing like the girls in grubby jeans who hung out at the barn mucking stalls, grooming horses, and cleaning tack.

The room began to fill up with classmates, riders from other barns, and a smattering of grownups. Girls in long gowns and fancy hairdos—barely recognizable from school—flirted with boys Kate hardly knew. Sue's older brother, Brad, appeared at her side.

"Hey," he said, handing her a pink balloon.

Kate blushed. She liked Brad. They'd hung out together at Halloween, and he'd asked her to be his date for Holly's party. She'd never really given him an answer, and Brad seemed cool with that. But it bothered Kate. She was supposed to be Nathan Crane's girlfriend—something a million girls would die for—so why did she feel all warm inside whenever Brad was around? It didn't make sense, at least not to her.

Boys, Kate thought, feeling awkward beside Brad. They're a whole lot more complicated than horses.

Adam waved his cell phone. "Heads up, everyone. Liz just called," he said. "Holly's on her way."

"Phew." Kate let out her breath. She'd almost convinced herself that Holly would have a meltdown over Adam's idiotic text and refuse to go out for dinner with her mom.

There was a mad dash for hiding places. People crouched beneath tables and jammed themselves into corners. Someone grabbed her hand, and Kate found herself standing between Sue and Jennifer at the reception desk. Robin was across the hall, lurking behind a coat rack.

"Duck," Jennifer said, and they hunkered down.

A car swept up the driveway, and headlights shone into the foyer. From where they hid, Kate could hear the engine of Liz's old van, running a little rough like it always did.

"She's here," Sue whispered.

Kate peeked around the counter as Holly pushed open the glass doors and slouched toward them with her head down. She looked more miserable than Kate had ever seen her.

3

An hour earlier, Holly had made a deal with her mother. She'd get dressed up and go out for dinner, but first they had to stop at the barn.

"Why?" Liz said.

Holly shrugged into her jacket. "Because I want to hug my horse."

Magician was the only one who knew how she felt. He listened and didn't argue or try to tell her what to do. He'd always been there for her, even when she couldn't walk and was stuck in a wheelchair and could only reach a few bits of him to groom.

The barn was dark except for a floodlight that always came on when anything tripped it, even a squirrel. Leaving her mom in the car, Holly slipped inside. Horses stamped their feet and rattled buckets as she walked past. She patted Tapestry's golden nose and let herself into Magician's stall. The black gelding's forelock fell over one eye as he turned toward her. His velvety nostrils fluttered with a deep, welcoming whicker.

"Hey, fella," Holly whispered.

Wrapping both arms around his neck, she buried her face in his long, silky mane and never wanted to let go. He'd carried her to victory in the show ring, taken her for trail rides, and thrilled her on the cross-country course. And after her accident, when she'd begun riding again, he'd plodded along as slowly and carefully as a plow horse, never putting a foot wrong.

"I love you," Holly said and fed him a carrot.

Magician nudged her with his soft, whiskery nose, and Holly didn't even care that his slobber ran down the front of her jacket and onto her skirt. She wiped it off and hugged him again.

But the euphoria didn't last.

Magician was the best horse in the world, but even he couldn't compensate for Adam being a total jerk and a best friend who let her down. Holly flopped back into her mom's van and sat there, feeling like an outcast while they drove to the club to pick up some stupid paperwork her mother had forgotten.

"Must I?" Holly said, when Liz asked her to run inside and find it.

"Yes." Holly's mom gave her a gentle push out the door.

Sighing, Holly trudged up the clubhouse path. She shoved the front door open and stepped inside. It was dark, darker than normal. The place felt deserted, which was odd for a Saturday night. She looked around for the receptionist Mom had told her to find, but all she could see was a shiny bell on the counter you were supposed to ring when nobody was there.

So Holly rang the bell and everything exploded.

"*Surprise*!" yelled a chorus of voices.

Blinded by spotlights, Holly blinked as her friends erupted like shooting stars. Laughing and squealing, they hugged her so hard, she thought for sure her ribs were going to snap.

Where's Adam? she thought. Is he part of this?

Her eyes swept the foyer and she spotted him leaning against the wall and looking mighty pleased with himself. He gave a lop-sided grin and blew her a kiss. Holly felt herself go weak at the knees. Was that a tux he was wearing . . . and a pink feather boa?

She tried to talk, but the words got stuck in her throat. Jennifer draped a silvery cloak around her shoulders, Kate placed a tiara on her head, and Robin parked a pair of enormous sunglasses on her nose. Amid cheers and laughter, they led her along the red carpet into a room filled with so much glitter that Holly's head began to spin. Sue held a fake microphone in front of her.

"Smile for the camera," said a deep voice.

Flashes went off, one after another.

Adam grabbed her hands and kissed her cheek, and everyone clapped. This was amazing. Holly pinched herself to make she wasn't dreaming. Open-mouthed, she looked from one friend to another and saw a rainbow of dazzling colors, shining eyes, and wall-to-wall grins.

And there were her mom and Kate's dad standing off to one side. Mom nodded and gave her a thumbs-up.

When did all this happen? The food, the fabulous decorations, the gorgeous outfits . . . and that mountain of gifts? How did I not know? Blushing madly, Holly turned to Kate.

"I'm sorry," she whispered.

Kate held out her little finger. "Best friends?"

"Forever," Holly said.

"There's more," Jennifer said. "Follow me."

* * *

Ten minutes later, Kate watched a radiant Holly emerge from the ladies' room. She'd freshened her makeup, tied her blond hair into an elaborate knot, and secured it with the tiara. The purple satin dress fit like it was made for her.

"Miss America," Sue whispered.

Robin sighed. "Princess for a day."

Someone cranked up the music. Flourishing his feather boa, Adam sauntered up to Holly and wrapped another boa around her neck. With a wink at Kate, he took Holly's arm and whisked her off to the dance floor. The silvery straps of her dress caught the light as he twirled her in circles like they were on *Dancing with the Stars*. More couples joined in and soon they were lost in the crush. Kate felt a tap on her shoulder.

"Wanna dance?" Brad said.

Kate shrugged. "Sure."

She kicked off her thrift shop sandals—they were pinching her toes—and danced barefoot with Brad. He seemed to know way more steps than she did.

The music switched to a slow number. Without missing a beat, Brad pulled her close and Kate found herself at eye level with his shirt pocket. Somewhere in the depths of her evening purse, Kate's cell phone buzzed. With all her friends and her dad at the party, it could only be one person.

Nathan, calling from New Zealand.

Feeling guilty, Kate let it go to voice mail. She'd text

him tomorrow. Right now, she wanted to enjoy herself with Brad. He was actually there, right in front of her, unlike Nathan who spent most of his life in faraway places.

The other girls envied her for having a movie star boyfriend. They thought it was glamorous and exciting, but they had no idea how tough it was. She'd never been on a real date with Nathan because the minute he showed his famous face in public, he was mobbed by legions of fans. Girls swooned and fainted at his feet.

But underneath it all, Nathan was an ordinary guy and that's what Kate liked about him. He'd grown up in Vermont and gone to school with Adam, until he got discovered by a talent scout and ended up as a teenage superstar.

She felt a pang of envy for Holly.

Adam didn't go to their school, but he lived close enough, plus he loved horses and rode like a dream—with a stack of ribbons and trophies to prove it. Tomorrow, he was trucking Domino, his half-Arabian pinto, to the barn so he and Holly could go trail riding. Just the two of them, together, like a real date.

"You hungry?" Brad said. His voice was surprisingly soft for such a tall guy, and his mop of sandy brown curls made him look younger than sixteen.

"Yeah, sure," Kate said, as her tummy rumbled. In all the excitement, she'd forgotten to eat lunch.

The music quieted down, and people drifted toward the food table. Kate filled a plate with raw veggies, potato chips, and Mrs. West's delicious mini quiches. Brad grabbed two sodas and filled a bag with popcorn. Sue helped herself to nachos and dip, then whispered in Kate's ear, "Be nice to my brother. He's big, but he bruises easy."

Kate swallowed hard. She knew how much Sue wanted her to date Brad. Just then, Holly skipped over, hanging onto Adam's arm. Her eyes sparkled, her tiara had gone missing, and her oversized sunglasses stuck out of Adam's pocket.

"Look what he gave me," she said.

Around her neck was a tiny gold horse's head on a slender gold chain. With its long forelock and perky ears, the horse was a dead ringer for Magician.

"Fabulous," Kate said, touching it.

Sue nodded. "Sweet."

"Awesome," said Robin.

Jennifer wafted past with one of Brad's snowboarding buddies. "Cool beans," she said.

Holly glanced at the pool. "Let's go swimming."

"Not after eating," Brad said.

"So we'll wait an hour."

"I'll race you," Adam said. "In the butterfly."

"You're on," Holly replied.

They sealed the deal with a fist bump, and Kate grinned because she knew Holly would win. When her legs were still paralyzed, swimming was her only exercise and she got seriously good at it. Even Kate couldn't beat her, and she'd been on the swim team at her old school.

The music started up again, some sort of old-fashioned number, like a waltz, and to Kate's astonishment, her father and Holly's mom took the floor.

"I never knew Dad could dance," she said.

Holly grinned. "Mom's got two left feet."

"So does my dad," Kate said, still staring at her father, looking debonair in his navy blazer and crisp white shirt. He'd even managed to get all the paint out of his beard.

Jennifer's parents joined in, then the Shapiros, and soon all the grown-ups were gliding across the dance floor to what Holly said was an old Elvis Presley song, "Can't Help Fallin' in Love."

Abruptly, the music changed.

Drums thumped and guitars wailed as Lady Gaga belted out her latest number. Holly teamed up with Brad, and Kate danced with Adam. A hunk of streaky blond hair flopped over his forehead and reminded her of Nathan. They looked so much alike that they'd often swapped clothes in school just to confuse their teachers. In the *Moonlight* movie, Adam had ridden as Nathan's stunt double. Even their green eyes and goofy grins were a perfect match. Kate felt herself slip into a goofy grin as well, remembering that Holly had asked her for a sleepover. Tonight.

"My turn," Holly said, cutting in.

They changed partners and Kate danced with Brad again. "Great party," he said. "It's going well."

Kate nodded. *Maybe a little too well.* She glanced around, looking for trouble, for any sign of Angela and Courtney. They were probably playing tennis on the indoor courts. But sooner or later, they'd show up for a swim or a dip in the hot tub, and nobody could stop them. They were club members, and Mrs. Dean ran the club.

Kate knew she was being paranoid, but Angela had always messed things up in the past. Granted, she'd concentrated on messing up Kate's life, not Holly's, but—

The music ground to a halt. A split second later, it speeded up again, so fast it was like Alvin and the Chipmunks—faster and faster until it screeched louder than tomcats on a back fence. Kate covered her ears. Then came a horrendous bang, followed by sparks. It happened so fast that Adam was only halfway to the sound booth when all the lights popped and went out.

Someone clicked on a flashlight, and Kate caught a glimpse of black hair, then blond, and a flash of yellow. She grabbed Holly's arm. "Did you see that?"

"No, what?"

"Over there." Kate pointed, but nothing remained —just a nasty suspicion she couldn't quite put her finger on.

The lights came back on, and Adam had no sooner gotten the sound system up and running when the fire alarm blared. The club manager and two assistants burst into the room.

Screams rang out. Kids ran for the door.

The manager held up his arms. "Don't panic. It's an electrical glitch, but we've got to evacuate. Follow me, and everything will be okay."

4

AN UNWELCOME VOICE hit Kate the minute she reached the foyer. "This is unacceptable," came Mrs. Dean's strident tones. "This ridiculous fire drill has just ruined my daughter's tennis match."

Behind her stood Angela and Courtney, looking not the least concerned about fire alarms and an army of kids rushing out the door. Smirking at Kate, Angela tossed a wave of coal black hair over one shoulder. Courtney giggled and twirled her designer racquet like a baton. Both cousins wore matching yellow tennis dresses.

"I *knew* it," Kate said, sniffing.

"What?" Holly said.

Kate sniffed again, but she didn't smell smoke. In fact, the only thing that smelled was Angela's expression, smirkier than ever. The manager, already flustered, tried to usher Mrs. Dean toward the door. She complained but got swept outside with the crowd.

Sirens wailed as fire trucks sped up the driveway. Firemen jumped out and raced into the clubhouse. Others began unrolling hoses. One of them handed Brad Piretti a yellow jacket with his name in reflective tape on the back. Kate had forgotten he was a junior volunteer.

The fire chief barked into a megaphone. "Keep calm, everyone, and keep back."

Parents hustled kids into cars and SUVs. Kate's father yanked open the back door of Liz's van and ordered the girls inside. Liz climbed into the driver's seat and fired up the engine.

"My gifts," Holly wailed. "They're—"

"We'll come and get them tomorrow," Liz said. She tapped her watch. "It's almost eleven. I think we've all had enough excitement for one night."

Clenching her fist, Kate said, "I bet it's a false alarm."

Liz didn't appear to have heard. She was talking to Kate's dad through the car window, but Holly leaned in close and whispered, "Angela?"

"I don't know. Maybe."

"But that's a crime," Holly said. "Isn't it?"

Kate nodded. Angela loved causing trouble, but would she go this far to wreck Holly's party? Maybe all she did was mess with the sound system, and it backfired. The alarm going off was an unexpected bonus. No wonder she'd looked so smug.

* * *

Holly lay on her bed and stared at the ceiling. Herds of wild mustangs raced across it. Her mother had stuck them up there when all Holly could do was lie around after her accident. She blew upward at the mobile above her night table. Its brightly painted horses twirled like a carousel.

Quietly, Kate said, "I'm sorry about your party. We should've invited Angela. Then she wouldn't have—"

"No," Holly said. "Even if you *had* invited her, she'd have found a way to trash it."

"She's such a bratface," Kate said, using Holly's favorite word for Angela.

"Yup," Holly said.

Holly had known Angela since kindergarten, and she hadn't changed a bit from the spoiled five-year-old who threw a tantrum if another kid got gold stars and she didn't. At the hunter pace last month, she'd cheated her way into the blue ribbon. But Kate and Holly had blown the whistle on her, and now Angela was bent on revenge.

Well, two could play that game.

"I'm gonna—" Holly sucked in her breath. "I'm gonna burn her stupid pom-poms. I'll tell Mrs. Dean she flunked her midterm algebra test, and I'll—"

"Pull the bobbles off her tennis socks?" Kate said. "C'mon, Holly, get serious. Whatever you do, it'll make you look like an idiot. Besides we've got no proof."

"That's what you always say."

"Angela's mean and selfish, but she's not stupid," Kate said, sounding far more sensible than Holly felt. "Look, it's pretty obvious she messed up the sound system."

"Yeah," Holly said. "She totally wrecked it."

"But I don't think she set off the fire alarm," Kate went on. "She's way too smart for that, and even if she did, her mother would cover it up."

Holly groaned. As usual, Kate was right. Angela wasn't stupid but her mother was. Mrs. Dean pushed Angela to win at all costs and if Angela failed, she got yelled at. Last winter Angela lost a downhill ski race by one second. Her mother erupted and told the officials their stopwatches were wrong. She made such a fuss that they declared the race a tie and Angela got her gold medal.

Kate's cell phone buzzed. Moments later, so did

Holly's. She read Adam's text and glanced at her best friend. From the look on Kate's face, she was talking to a boy, but which one?

Nathan or Brad?

* * *

Adam and Holly were about to go trail riding when Brad walked into the barn wearing jeans and brown field boots that laced up the front. Trying not to feel flustered, Kate secured Tapestry to the crossties and concentrated on grooming her, even though she was superclean and didn't really need it.

What was Brad doing here?

He hadn't said a word about coming to the barn when he called her last night. Brad was an extreme snowboarder, not a rider. As far as Kate knew, he'd never even sat on a horse.

"Where'd you get those boots, dude?" Adam said.

Brad grinned. "My grandfather."

"He was master of the Winfield hunt," said Sue, coming up behind him. She still had a couple of tiny roses in her hair and a smudge of green shadow over one eye.

"There's a hunt in Winfield?" Kate said.

"Not anymore." Sue said with a shudder. "I *hate* fox hunting."

"I'm sorry about your party," Brad said to Holly. "The fire chief is pretty sure it was a circuit breaker that blew out, so no big deal."

Holly's eyes narrowed. She edged Magician closer to Kate and leaned down to whisper, "I wonder how much Mrs. Dean paid him to say that."

"Don't be an idiot," Kate replied. "You can't bribe the fire department."

Domino whinnied and tossed his head, as if impatient to get going. Adam wheeled him around and headed for the door. In his knapsack, he'd told Kate in secret, was a picnic lunch for him and Holly to share on the trail.

Most of the snow from the blizzard they'd had just after Halloween had melted from the lower slopes, but there was still plenty at the peak, thanks to the Timber Ridge snow guns. Kate was kind of surprised Brad wasn't up there, shredding the half-pipe or whatever it was that snowboarders did.

After Holly and Adam trotted off, Brad said, "Sue's gonna teach me to ride."

"On Tara?" Kate said. Sue's mare was barely fifteen hands. Her brother's long legs would drag on the ground.

"No," Sue said, laughing. "On Marmalade. He's big enough."

He was certainly calm enough for a beginner. The seventeen-hand chestnut rarely moved faster than a walk. He was part Percheron and part something else, except nobody knew what it was.

"Bulldozer, probably," Liz always said.

Sue got busy showing Brad how to groom Marmalade, and Kate was almost finished with Tapestry when the barn door slid open and in walked Angela. She wore buff breeches and a yellow parka the same shade as her tennis dress. Behind her came Courtney wearing skin-tight jeans, purple sneakers, and white socks with pink bobbles. Kate's fingers itched to pluck them off.

Angela sauntered down the aisle. "Nice party last night."

"Yeah," Courtney drawled. "Pity it was so short."

"But they had *great* dresses," Angela said.

"From the Salvation Army," Courtney said, twirling a strand of blond hair. "It's *the* place for fashion."

Sue stuck her head out of Marmalade's stall and stared at Courtney's spotless pink hoodie. "So, you gonna groom Skywalker for Angela, then?" she said.

Kate stifled a laugh. Angela never groomed her own horse. Her younger step-sister had always done the dirty work, but Marcia was now living in New York with her father, who rarely came home to Timber Ridge. Kate wasn't sure Angela even knew how to groom Skywalker. He stood in his stall, terminally bored, because Angela refused to allow him outside in the paddock. He'd already chewed his door to bits and was halfway through eating his windowsill as well.

Brad held up a curry comb. "I'll do it."

"Don't you dare," Sue warned.

"Only kidding."

Angela simpered. "Oh, Brad. Would you? That would be so cool."

"Forget it," Sue snapped. "Brush your own horse."

With a dismissive snort, Angela grabbed her cousin's arm and dragged her into the tack room. Moments later they emerged carrying a saddle and bridle—but no grooming box—and disappeared into Skywalker's stall. From the sounds of it, Angela wasn't much good at tacking up her horse, either. When she finally led him into the aisle, Kate could see that his girth was twisted.

"You might want to fix that," she said. "And his martingale. It's way too tight."

Angela ignored her. She stood on the mounting box, climbed awkwardly into her saddle, and clattered off toward the barn's indoor arena with Courtney trailing behind. Kate decided to use the outside ring instead.

Sharing the indoor with Angela would be a challenge. Skywalker hadn't been ridden in two weeks and would probably explode like a loose cannon. How on earth Angela hoped to be ready for the horse show tryouts, Kate couldn't imagine.

Aunt Bea—Liz's old riding instructor—would pick the team over Thanksgiving weekend. Liz refused to do it herself now that Holly was riding again.

"If I picked my own daughter, I'd be accused of favoritism," she declared. "We need someone with an unbiased opinion."

What she didn't mention was that if she chose the team and failed to include Angela, Mrs. Dean would have a major meltdown and threaten to fire her.

The next show was small but crucial. It was the first of several qualifying events that counted toward the Festival of Horses in April where, it was rumored, scouts from the U.S. Equestrian Team would be on the lookout for young riding talent.

Kate was determined to qualify.

So was Holly.

Angela claimed not to care, but Kate knew better. Mrs. Dean was counting on Angela winning, just so she could show off to her fancy friends that Angela was an equestrian superstar.

"My daughter's headed for the next Olympics," Angela's mother would boast to anyone who'd listen.

In a way, Kate felt almost sorry for Angela. What must it be like to have a mom who only loved you for the gold medals and blue ribbons you won? Maybe if Angela had a different mother, she'd be—

Tapestry snorted and danced sideways.

Kate gathered up her reins and headed for the outdoor ring. Sue was already in there, leading Brad at a sedate walk. He appeared to have a natural seat and good balance, probably because of all the snowboarding he did. His back was straight and his hands quiet, and he wore a confident smile. Then Sue ruined the illusion by urging Marmalade into a slow trot, and poor Brad flopped about like a gigantic sock puppet.

Keeping out of his way, Kate warmed up at the far end of the ring. She trotted and cantered Tapestry in circles, did a few half halts, and popped over the brush jump. The double oxer and parallel bars beckoned, so she jumped those as well.

Tapestry flicked her ears back and forth like antennae, listening to Kate and waiting for the next signal. Feeling brave, Kate aimed Tapestry at the chicken coop, her least favorite jump. Tapestry tried to run out, but Kate was expecting that and kept her in a straight line.

The mare tucked her front legs and cleared the coop with inches to spare.

Sue applauded. "Way to go."

"Awesome," Brad said, and tipped his riding helmet.

As they plodded along the rail, Marmalade closed one eye like he was winking at Kate. Then Brad did the same, and Kate smiled. It was kind of cool having a guy in the ring even if he was a rank beginner who'd never want to ride again once he found out how much it hurt.

Brad was an athlete, but Kate was willing to bet he'd never used those particular leg muscles before, and boy, were they going to complain tomorrow morning. He'd probably show up at school on crutches.

Grinning to herself, Kate gave Tapestry a loose rein and thought how odd it was that you rarely saw boys learning to ride, but when it came to international horse shows and three-day events, half the competitors were men. Did they learn to ride in secret or in a special camp just for boys . . . no girls allowed?

Adam was the only boy her age Kate knew who loved horses and riding as much as she did. But he rode for a competing team. Holly was always teasing him about that, telling him he ought to switch sides and ride for Timber Ridge instead.

But only residents of Timber Ridge could ride for the team. Mrs. Dean made sure of that. She didn't want too much competition for Angela.

5

THE TRAIL WIDENED, so Holly urged Magician forward and rode alongside Adam. With a shy smile, he held out his hand and Holly took it. His warm fingers curled around hers.

Could it get any better than this?

They'd already shared cheese roll-ups, peanut butter cookies, and a bottle of root beer, and now they were riding side-by-side through a leafy glade—well, it would've been leafy a few months earlier—just like the scenes in *Moonlight*, her favorite fantasy novel.

Holly's imagination ran wild.

Magical light streamed through the trees. Bluebirds chirped and butterflies fluttered. Sitting cross-legged on moonbeams the size of raindrops, pixies floated down to a nest of dewy grass where rabbits frolicked amid tufts of buttercups and daisies. Iridescent fairies spread their gossamer wings, and through the silvery mist came a cake frosted with snowflakes and stars. Holly counted fifteen tiny candles.

"Happy Birthday," the fairies trilled, their voices sweet as sugarplums. Waving sparkly wands, they conjured up a giant bumble bee. It flew toward Holly. Closer and closer it buzzed. It sounded just like—

Adam's cell phone.

He let go of Holly's hand to answer it. Her fantasy dissolved. Thanks to Angela, she hadn't gotten to blow out her candles last night.

"You're not gonna like this," Adam said as he stuffed the phone in his pocket.

Domino spooked at a rock. He arched his neck and acted as if he'd never seen anything like it before. Ears pricked, he snorted and skittered sideways. Adam patted his shoulder. "Easy, boy."

"What won't I like?" Holly said.

"Kristina James," Adam replied. "My trainer just said she's moving to Timber Ridge."

Holly's heart sank. "When?"

"Next week."

"Ugh," Holly said, pretending to retch.

Kristina rode for the Larchwood team. She'd been throwing herself at Adam ever since they won the hunter pace last month. After the awards ceremony, she'd even kissed him. Holly had wanted to slap her. Kristina was also best friends with Angela, another strike against her.

Adam grinned. "My loss, your gain."

"Beast," Holly said and wanted to slap him as well.

* * *

Kate's mouth fell open when Holly dropped the bombshell about Kristina James. "You have got to be kidding."

"Nope," Holly said. She ran a cloth over Magician's sweaty neck and rubbed between his forelegs. He tucked his head, pulled the cloth from her hands, and waved it like a surrender flag.

Despite herself, Kate laughed. Trust Magician to defuse a tense situation. It was as if he knew when they needed to lighten up.

"Our team will now have seven members," Holly went on, not making Kate feel any better. "Plus, Kristina's moving into the house across from Angela."

That was the one Kate had picked out for her and Dad.

Oh well, they couldn't have afforded it anyway. They'd have to find something a whole lot smaller if they wanted to live at Timber Ridge. Trouble was, all the houses were huge. Holly called them McMansions. Some had three-car garages, indoor pools, and high-tech security systems wired directly into the local police station.

But with Kristina moving into the neighborhood, Liz would have more riders to choose from. And if Mrs. Dean put her weight behind the newcomer, Kristina was sure to make the team.

Except *Aunt Bea* was picking this team. She would not play favorites. She'd ignore Mrs. Dean and choose the best riders. She'd even overlook Holly and Kate if they didn't measure up.

For the next week, Kate spent every spare minute at the barn, putting Tapestry through her paces, listening to Liz and learning as much as possible. She was determined to pass Aunt Bea's rigorous tests. One of them, she'd heard, would be written.

* * *

"Not fair," Angela complained, when Liz handed out details of the upcoming event. "I want to ride, not answer dumb questions."

"Get used to it," Liz said. "If you qualify for the final, it'll include a two-hour written test, and it'll be a lot tougher than anything Bea Parker comes up with."

"When's she coming?" Kate whispered to Holly.

They were all crammed into Liz's small office. Sue and Robin shared a tack trunk, Jennifer perched on the filing cabinet, and Angela was leaning against the doorframe beside Kristina James, who'd shown up at the barn that morning with Cody, her palomino Quarter Horse.

"Wednesday night," Holly said, shifting over to make room for Kate on the sawhorse. "She's going to cook Thanksgiving dinner, too. I said we'd help."

Kate heaved a sigh of relief.

Her dad and Holly's mom were hopeless in the kitchen. They'd planned on having Thanksgiving dinner at the Winfield Tavern until Aunt Bea vetoed the idea and volunteered to cook the turkey herself.

"What sort of questions will be on the test?" Robin said.

Liz looked thoughtful for a moment, then said, "What's the difference between a paint and a pinto?"

"Spelling?" Holly said.

Everyone groaned.

Kate said, "Adam's horse is a half-Arabian, and he's black-and-white. So what is he?" There was also Daisy, mostly white with a few black patches. She'd been Magician's best friend until Tapestry came along and he'd fallen in love with her instead.

"A tobiano?" Sue said. "Or an overo?"

Robin threw up her hands. "I can't tell the difference."

"Then hit the web and find out," Liz said. "You already know most of this stuff, so don't panic, okay?"

Angela scowled and jabbed her finger at the list Liz had given her. "What's all this about tack and turnout?"

"Yeah," chimed in Kristina. She pushed a lock of chestnut brown hair off her face. "It's got something about stable management as well. Don't we have grooms for that?"

"Not in this barn," Liz said, pinning her with a look. "You do your own work—grooming, mucking stalls, and cleaning your tack. *All* of it. No skimping on halters and lead ropes, either." She paused. "You'll be judged on all of this at the finals, so be prepared."

"Worse than the stupid Pony Club," Kristina muttered.

"Then don't try out," Holly said, in a sickly sweet voice. "Nobody's forcing you."

Angela crumpled Liz's list and stuffed it into her pocket. Then she grabbed Kristina's arm and hauled her off to see Skywalker. In the adjacent stall stood Cody, looking wild-eyed and restless in his new home. He tossed his head, snatched a mouthful of hay, and stuck his nose over the door. Kate admired his pale cream forelock and the blaze that ran down his face.

Blaze, stripe, star, and snip.

Those might be questions on the written test.

* * *

Kate doubled up her riding practice. So did Holly. They rode twice a day, both on the flat and over the indoor jump course. They devoured back issues of *Dressage Today* and *Chronicle of the Horse*. Taking turns, they quizzed each other on conformation, breeds, and genetics.

"What color horse do you get when you cross a chestnut with a cremello?" Kate said.

Holly frowned. "A palomino?"

"Right," Kate said. "And what color eyes does a cremello have?"

"Blue, I think."

Kate nodded. "Yes."

"Okay, my turn," Holly said. "What's a grulla?"

"Some sort of doughnut?"

"That's a cruller, you idiot," Holly said.

"No, it's that awful woman from *101 Dalmatians*," Kate said, "the one with all the spotted fur coats." She knew what a grulla was—a dun-colored horse with a dorsal stripe—but she wanted to tease her best friend.

Holly rolled her eyes. "Cruella de Vil."

"Yeah," Kate said, shuddering.

With a grin, Holly declared this was more fun than choosing nail polish. She fired up her laptop and they cruised the web to research breeds and colors and the many variations of dun, buckskin, and roan. Digging further, they learned about Fjords and Icelandic horses and how all modern horses evolved from tiny *Eohippus* that had lived 50 million years ago.

"I bet Angela doesn't know this stuff," Holly said. "She never studies for anything."

"Maybe she's relying on Kristina for help," Kate said. Kristina had officially joined the Timber Ridge team and would be another contender for the next event. Three spots open and seven girls trying out.

Kate crossed her fingers and hoped nothing would prevent Aunt Bea from showing up. The last time Liz invited Aunt Bea to pick the team, a last-minute book tour sent her in another direction, and they wound up with Angela's private trainer choosing the team instead. He was long gone, but Kate wouldn't put it past Angela or her mother to complain about Aunt Bea.

* * *

Bea Parker arrived on Wednesday afternoon, complete with her laptop, a turkey baster, and two copies of her latest thriller.

"First things first," Aunt Bea said, dumping cookbooks and roasting pans on Liz's kitchen table. "I want to see Kate's new horse."

Proudly, Kate showed her off.

She'd rescued Tapestry from a dealer who trucked unwanted horses to Canada and Mexico for slaughter. At first, Kate had no idea what a treasure she'd bought, but when the layers of grime and old hair fell away, Tapestry's copper-colored coat and her flaxen mane and tail had turned her into a showstopper.

Kate had posted photos on Facebook, and three weeks later, Tapestry's former owner, Richard North, recognized his missing mare and got in touch. Her old name was Serenade and she was a registered Morgan who'd been stolen from his farm almost a year before. He was so relieved that Tapestry was alive and being taken care of that he'd gifted her to Kate with the proviso that when Kate went to college, she would breed Tapestry to Maestro, his award-winning stallion, and Mr. North would get first refusal on the foal.

Holly had already dubbed it Arpeggio.

"She's gorgeous," Aunt Bea said, running her expert's hands down Tapestry's well-muscled shoulders and across her back. "I bet she's a good dressage horse."

"And a jumper," Holly chimed in. "She cleared the paddock fence."

"With Kate?" Aunt Bea raised one ginger-colored eyebrow. It matched her gingery-red curls that reminded Kate of Ms. Frizzle in *The Magic School Bus.*

"By herself," Kate said, grinning.

"Well, then," said Aunt Bea. "I can't wait to see you guys in action."

* * *

On Thanksgiving morning, Aunt Bea banished Liz and Kate's father, Ben, to the living room. "You can swap stories about butterflies and horses," she said, handing them mugs of coffee. "The girls and I will make dinner."

Kate rinsed broccoli and Holly diced carrots while Aunt Bea stuffed the turkey and whipped up an apple pie. Its tantalizing smell wafted out of the kitchen and prompted Kate's dad to stick his head around the door.

"Can I have some right now?"

Aunt Bea shooed him out.

"Your folks make a nice couple," she said, after closing the door.

Kate grinned at Holly. That's what they both thought. In fact, they'd been quietly conspiring to get their parents together—on their own, without kids hanging around. They'd come up with a dozen different ideas, but they were all wickedly expensive. No way could they afford to send Ben and Liz on a romantic Caribbean cruise or to buy them tickets for a Broadway show.

"Cooking lessons," Aunt Bea said.

Holly opened her mouth and shut it again.

"Hear me out," said Aunt Bea, basting the turkey. "There's an adult ed cooking course at the high school. Your folks need it, and I'll help you pay for it. Sign them up and give them gift certificates for Christmas, okay?" She banged the oven door shut. "Your parents can bond over slicing onions and selecting spices for a curry."

"Yum," Kate said. "Chicken tikka masala."

With a knowing smile, Aunt Bea dusted flour off her hands and popped a sweet potato casserole in the microwave.

6

To Kate's surprise, Mrs. Dean invited the riding team to use her family room for their written test on Friday afternoon. Aunt Bea had banned all electronic devices—no cell phones, iPads, or laptops allowed—and asked Mrs. Dean to turn off the wifi.

"This is a *real* test," she said. "I want to know how much you know, not how well you can surf the web."

The girls spread themselves out on couches, chairs, and footstools. Mrs. Dean provided green pencils and matching clipboards with *Timber Ridge* written in gold script across the top.

"I bet the room is bugged," Holly whispered.

"Why?" Kate said.

"So she can signal the answers to Angela. She's probably wearing a hidden device." Holly stared at their rival, as if expecting to see wires sticking out of her ears.

"You read too much science fiction," Kate said.

It was impossible to relax. The Deans' family room was filled with antique furniture, oriental rugs, and crystal bowls on spindly tables. Kate was afraid to move in case she knocked something over. Hanging above the fireplace was an enormous portrait of Angela in a classical dressage outfit—shadbelly coat, yellow vest, and top hat—even though she'd never ridden beyond first level.

"There are twenty questions," Aunt Bea said, passing them out. "You may answer a maximum of ten, so choose wisely and do the best you can. Question number one is the easiest and is worth one point. Question two is worth two points, and so on."

Robin frowned. "So if we answer questions eleven through twenty we'll get the most points?"

"Yes," Aunt Bea said, "providing you get them all right." With a smile, she ran a hand through her wiry curls and looked more like Ms. Frizzle than ever. "And in case you're wondering, the highest possible score is one hundred fifty-five."

Kate scanned the first three questions.

List the competitions that make up a three-day event.

Define a hunter pace.

Name four different snaffle bits.

They were super easy but they were only worth a total of six points. "How long have we got?" she said.

"One hour," Aunt Bea replied. "You may begin now."

From a quilted tote bag, she pulled out her knitting and an oven timer that she parked on the mantel. It began ticking right away. After handing Mrs. Dean a test paper, Aunt Bea settled down in a rocking chair with her latest sock creation. Immediately, Angela's mother began to read. Her lips moved silently like a kid who was still learning to form words.

Was this a signal to Angela?

Of course not. Mrs. Dean didn't know one end of a horse from the other . . . unless her test paper also had the answers. Kate tried to concentrate, but she couldn't help glancing at Mrs. Dean. Maybe she was just telling Angela *Good luck* or, more likely, *Don't mess it up.*

Pulling her scattered wits together, Kate scanned the questions again and decided to begin with number eleven: *What's the difference between a standing and a running martingale?* Kate scribbled her answer then tackled question twelve: *Name the three foundation sires of the Thoroughbred breed.* Okay, she knew that one, too, thanks to all the research she and Holly had done.

The questions got steadily tougher and Kate found herself stumped by number fifteen: Equus *means what in Greek?* She gave it thirty seconds and moved on. A quick glance at the others showed they were struggling, too. Only Angela and Kristina wore confident expressions.

Having given up on number fifteen, Kate back-tracked to number ten: *Name three grand-prix dressage movements*. Easy-peasy.

Piaffe, passage, and pirouette.

Then came: *Define colic and list recommended treatments*. That was followed by a fill-in-the-blank conformation chart and questions about hoof ailments. Kate looked at her watch. Fifty minutes down; another ten to go. She double-checked her answers and tackled number fifteen again, but it eluded her.

It was almost a relief when Aunt Bea said, "Time's up."

"Phew," Jennifer said. "That was rugged."

"I totally blew it," said Sue.

Robin sighed. "What's a hinny?"

"A cross between a stallion and a female donkey," Kristina said, smiling like a cat that had just swallowed a canary. She shot Robin a look that said she was dumber than a post for not knowing it.

Aunt Bea cleared her throat. "Okay, girls. I'll see

you all tomorrow morning. Nine o'clock, indoor arena. We'll do a dressage test first, then jumping in the outside ring."

"Dressage test?" Angela said. "Which one?"

"Mine," Aunt Bea said. "Just a basic walk, trot, and canter with smooth transitions and rounded circles. After that, you can add anything else you're comfortable with—half-passes and extensions; a flying change if you can swing it."

"Seriously?" Jennifer said.

Aunt Bea smiled. "Feel free to impress me."

* * *

Nathan texted at midnight. It was five o'clock on Saturday afternoon in New Zealand. He was at a sidewalk café waiting for friends to join him. Kate yawned and wished he wasn't so far away.

I miss you, he wrote.

Kate hesitated before writing, *Me, too.*

He asked about Thanksgiving, then sent her links to YouTube videos of where they'd been filming—jagged mountains and dark, mysterious caves that Nathan said were filled with knee-high crystals and underground streams. It looked wild and remote, and Kate didn't know what to say. Nathan's world was light years away from hers, like on another planet. Last week's fan magazine had him and Tess O'Donnell on the cover—yet again—and Holly had tried to hide it, but Kate saw it anyway.

They'd been through this before.

Nathan insisted it was just studio PR, and Kate believed him. But it was hard to take when the kids at school stuck photos of him and Tess on her locker and hummed the theme from *Moonlight* whenever she walked by.

Angela was the worst.

She loved nothing more than rubbing Kate's nose in Nathan's well-publicized glamour shots, especially the ones of him and his co-star. Last week she'd posted a photo on her Facebook page of Nathan and Tess wearing dark glasses and holding hands outside a nightclub. Beneath it she'd written: *Guess who'll be jealous over this!*

Kate shook her head to clear it. She texted Nathan with news about the horse show and Aunt Bea's test.

Did you ace it? he asked.

Dunno, Kate replied.

There was a pause, then came, *Gotta go*, and Kate had visions of Tess O'Donnell—blue eyes, pouty lips, and blond hair—sauntering up to Nathan and smothering him with kisses while the paparazzi snapped pictures that would be all over the web in a couple of hours.

* * *

The girls drew straws and Jennifer ended up riding first. The others sat on their horses in the center of the arena while Aunt Bea called out instructions. Liz watched from the observation room with Mrs. Dean and a hawk-faced woman who was probably Kristina's mother. Kate had never seen her before.

At Aunt Bea's command, Jennifer walked, trotted, and cantered. She crossed the diagonal at an extended trot and made a perfectly round twenty-meter circle, followed by two impressive flying changes. Rebel pricked his ears and looked as if he were enjoying himself.

"Nice ride," Aunt Bea said.

She made notes on her clipboard and told Robin to go next. Chantilly seemed half-asleep. She stumbled a few times and stuck her nose in the air when Robin asked her to back up. Then Kristina took the rail with Cody. Smoothly, he transitioned from walk to canter and changed leads when Kristina gave the signal with aids so subtle, Kate almost missed them.

"She's good," Holly muttered.

Reluctantly, Kate agreed. Kristina James was sure to make the team unless Cody fell apart over the jump course, which was highly unlikely, given how well he'd performed at the Labor Day horse show and last month's hunter pace.

"You're next, Sue," Aunt Bea announced.

As Sue guided Tara through Aunt Bea's required movements, Kate realized something was off. Sue's hands were stiff and her back was rigid, and she lost her stirrups when Tara shied at a traffic cone she'd seen a million times before.

"Rotten luck," Kate said.

Sue gave a little shrug. "Whatever."

"Look at Magician," Robin said. "He's showing off."

Neck arched and tail flagged, Holly's horse danced his way around the arena, like he knew everyone was watching. Well, except for Angela and Kristina. They were too busy talking to pay attention. They missed Holly's flying change, her flawless shoulder-in, and an extended trot where Magician's feet barely seemed to touch the ground.

Kate said. "That was awesome."

"Only awesome?" Holly said, grinning.

"Epic, then."

Leaning forward, Holly flung her arms around Magician's neck. She dropped a dozen kisses up and down his mane. "Isn't he amazing?"

"He's triple fantabulous," Kate said, meaning it.

She loved Magician as much as she loved Tapestry. He was the first horse she'd ridden at Timber Ridge. Together, they'd helped Liz's team beat Larchwood to win the Hampshire County challenge cup.

Holly pulled off the riding gloves Kate had given her. "I love these," she said, handing them to Kate. "They're soooo comfortable. Try them."

"Thanks." Kate slipped them on as Aunt Bea called Angela's name. Skywalker jiggled his bit. Gobs of foam flew from his mouth and landed on his sweaty shoulders.

"Time to watch Princess Angela flub up," Holly said. "She hasn't practiced in weeks."

But Skywalker didn't put a foot wrong. Neither did Angela. She posted on the proper diagonal, cantered on the correct lead, and managed a graceful half-pass, which was a first. Kate had never seen Skywalker do that before. Had they been practicing in secret? Then again, he was a push-button horse, and Angela had just pushed all the right buttons.

"Not bad," Kate said.

Holly scowled. "More like dumb luck."

Trying not to feel nervous, Kate waited for Aunt Bea's signal. She glanced at the observation room. Mrs. Dean and the other woman had disappeared, but Liz was still there. She gave a slight nod, and Kate's tension rose another notch. At all costs, she had to keep her hands calm and not let her anxiety travel down the reins to Tapestry's mouth.

* * *

After it was over, Kate could barely remember what she'd done, but it must've been okay because Holly gave her a high five and Jennifer punched the air with her fist.

Angela scowled and rode off.

"That was a lovely ride," said Aunt Bea, patting Tapestry. "Now, you can all take a break while Liz and I set up the jumps. I'll see you in the outside ring after lunch."

Kate led Tapestry into her stall, fed her two carrots and a small flake of hay, and removed her tack. After checking to make sure the mare was thoroughly cooled off, Kate lugged her saddle and bridle to the tack room where Holly was buffing her stirrups. Aunt Bea had warned them she'd be judging them on turnout as well as jumping.

Kate had just finished soaping her bridle when Angela stormed through the door, waving her newest iPod.

"Okay, who took them?" she said.

Holly sighed. "Took what?"

"My ear buds," Angela snapped. "They're gone."

"Again?" Kate said.

Last week, she'd found Angela's ear buds draped over a faucet in the wash bay. Before that, it was Angela's curling iron that went missing. She'd accused Kate of stealing it and didn't even apologize when it turned up in Mrs. Dean's car.

Without answering, Angela shook out horse blankets, upended buckets, and rummaged through grooming boxes. Her pale blue eyes swept the tack room like searchlights, back and forth over the double row of saddle racks.

"Give it up," Kate said. "They're not here."

"Wrong!" Angela shrieked and snatched her ear buds off Holly's bridle peg. "I *knew* it," she said, waving them in Holly's face. "*You* took them."

"Yeah, whatever," Holly said, rolling her eyes. "And I was dumb enough to leave them in full view?"

Angela seemed about to argue when Kristina yelled at her to hurry up. Mrs. Dean was waiting. Stuffing the errant ear buds in her pocket, Angela flounced off, leaving Kate with an uneasy feeling.

Holly had lost her own ear buds last week and hadn't replaced them. But no, that was crazy. She wouldn't have taken Angela's to get even for messing up her party.

Would she?

7

AN HOUR LATER, Kate and Holly tacked up their horses and rode into the outdoor ring. One by one, Sue, Robin, and Jennifer joined them. Then Aunt Bea arrived, five minutes ahead of Angela and Kristina, and she bawled them out for being late. Wearing identical scowls, they got in line with the others.

Nobody escaped Aunt Bea's criticism, including Robin who'd even polished the buckles on her bridle. They sparkled like tiny silver charms amid the brown leather straps.

After being scolded for a loose girth, Kate couldn't help smiling as Liz's old riding instructor, armed with a knitting needle, poked saddle soap out of the holes in Cody's throatlatch and told Angela that her martingale was too tight. With eagle-eyed scrutiny, Aunt Bea lifted flaps, adjusted keepers, and wiped dust off riders' boots.

"Always carry a cloth," she said, shaking out hers. "Wipe your boots before you go into the ring, or get someone else to do it for you."

Kristina leaned toward Angela and whispered, "She's worse than a drill sergeant with white gloves."

"I heard that, young lady," Aunt Bea said, spinning around. "And I'll take it as a compliment." She tucked her clipboard beneath one arm. "Okay, same order as before. Jennifer, you go first, please."

Aunt Bea and Liz had set up seven jumps, none higher than three feet, and spread out evenly over a figure-eight course. The most difficult was the final obstacle—a tricky combination that had two strides between the parallel bars and a double oxer.

Kate heaved a quiet sigh of relief.

Clearly, the chicken coop wasn't part of Aunt Bea's plan because she'd just dumped her quilted tote bag on it. From the top of the bag poked a large ball of multicolored yarn skewered with wooden needles. Aunt Bea's toe socks were legendary. She'd given Holly a pair for her birthday—hot pink, lime green, and neon orange stripes—and promised to give Holly knitting lessons the next time she came to stay.

With no trouble, Jennifer and Rebel cleared Aunt

Bea's course. Then came Robin and she did really well, much better than her dressage routine that morning. But Kristina misjudged the hogsback and Cody put in an extra stride. Jumping awkwardly, he sent the top rail flying, and Kristina jerked his mouth. Aunt Bea frowned and jabbed her clipboard so hard with her pencil that she broke its tip.

Kate wished Sue good luck and crossed her fingers. Tara cleared one obstacle after another, until she demolished the wall's top row of bricks. Then it was Holly's turn and Kate crossed her fingers even harder. But she needn't have worried. Magician was a pro. For him, these fences were child's play—no more of a challenge than the toy jumps in Holly's model horse collection.

Skywalker was already lathered up by the time Angela approached the first jump. Ears pinned, he leaped over the crossrail like an angry cat and almost unseated his rider. Angela grabbed his mane and shoved herself back into the saddle in time to tackle the brush jump. Somehow, they managed to clear the rest of the course, but Aunt Bea didn't look too impressed by their performance.

"Your turn, Kate," she said.

A knot of anxiety made a one-way trip from Kate's brain to her hands on Tapestry's reins, but Tapestry ignored it. She knew what she was doing. Without waiting for Kate's signal, Tapestry cantered toward the crossrail, cleared it, and bounded over the brush jump. Finally, Kate caught up with her brilliant horse and by the time they reached the three-bar gate, Kate was back in control.

One, two, three . . . and up.

Tapestry soared over it with room to spare.

The hogsback loomed—a fearsome jump with three rails, the highest one in the middle. With little effort, Tapestry cleared that as well. Kate curved right, toward the wall which was flanked by white wings and window boxes filled with faded plastic flowers. Tapestry gathered herself up and soared over the wall like a big, golden bird. Kate felt as if they were flying.

Landing safely, they headed for the combination. Kate was sure her heart was almost in her mouth. She held Tapestry back, then let her go—over the parallel bars, two strides, followed by the double oxer.

Kate flung her arms around Tapestry's neck. "I love you," she whispered into the mare's flaxen mane. They trotted toward the others.

Aunt Bea shot Kate a brief smile. "You've all done a great job, and I'm impressed with your hard work." There was a short pause while she rummaged in her tote bag. "I seem to be missing a couple of needles," she said, frowning. "But no worries. I have plenty more at home."

With that, she strode off. She handed her clipboard to Liz and climbed into her old red Subaru. Kate hated to see her go. Life was always more exciting when Aunt Bea was around.

* * *

Holly didn't want to go back to the barn. She was too restless. So was Magician. Arching his neck, he jogged in place. It was almost like riding a Grand Prix dressage horse. For a wild and crazy moment, Holly pretended she was in the Olympics: *She wore a top hat and shad-belly coat; Magician's saddle pad displayed the stars and stripes. Crowds cheered as they accepted the gold medal, and—*

Magician snorted at a fence post and brought Holly back to earth. "Let's go for a ride," she said.

"Sure," Kate replied. "But when's your mom going to announce the team?"

"Later this afternoon," Holly said, wheeling Magician away from the barn and toward the trail she'd taken with Adam. It was super cool riding with Kate, but it was extra special when she rode with Adam. She wished he was with them—right now—but he was at *his* barn, practicing for the same event they were. The

Larchwood team was really strong, even without Kristina James. Holly wondered who'd taken her place.

"Who do you think will make it?" Kate said.

"On Adam's team?" Holly said, still thinking about her boyfriend. So far, they'd competed against each other twice. Holly had beaten him in a jump-off at the Labor Day show, but he and Kristina James had won blue at the hunter pace.

Kate laughed. "No, silly. Ours."

"Jennifer, definitely. She was awesome, and I bet her written test was, too, even if she did moan about it."

"You'll be on it for sure," Kate said.

"So will you," Holly said, feeling bad about Robin and Sue. They were both good riders, but sometimes it came down to luck and what sort of mood your horse was in. Neither Tara nor Chantilly had cooperated today.

"What about Kristina?" Kate went on.

"Didn't you see the way she jerked Cody's mouth? I thought Aunt Bea was going to slam her, big time," Holly said.

"Okay," Kate said. "So where does that leave Angela?"

Holly grinned. "In the dust?"

"She's not gonna be happy," Kate said. "Neither is her mother."

As far as Holly could remember, Angela had always made the riding team, except for the Labor Day show when she dropped out and rode for Larchwood instead. It didn't last, and she was back at Timber Ridge two weeks later. But even though the next event was small, just a qualifying show, it was hugely important. If you didn't qualify, you couldn't ride in the Festival of Horses next April.

Angela failed to qualify last year.

This time, Holly knew that Mrs. Dean would pull whatever strings needed pulling in order for Angela to make it.

Magician tossed his head. "Okay, okay," Holly said, hauling her mind away from Angela and her miserable mother. She glanced at Kate. Tapestry was jigging about, as eager to run as Magician. "Let's go."

Leaves crunched beneath the horses' hooves as they cantered along the wide open trail. Ahead lay the hunt course. Less than a month ago it had been covered in two feet of snow. It's where they'd found Marcia Dean after she ran away with her sister's horse. Marcia had fallen off Skywalker and broken her collar bone, so Kate had stayed with her while Holly rode off to get help. Marcia's father, an investment banker, had been so grateful that he'd helped Kate's father buy the butterfly museum.

"It's the least I can do," Mr. Dean had told them.

Marcia was an odd little kid and Holly missed her around the barn. But she was now living with her dad in Manhattan and rumor had it that the Deans were getting a divorce. Angela, of course, denied it. So did her mother. Mrs. Dean acted like she always did—lording it over tennis tournaments, charity horse shows, and bridge parties as if she were the queen of Timber Ridge.

* * *

Liz was waiting in her office when Kate and Holly got back to the barn. All the others were there, including Angela who said, "I am *so* sick of you guys being late."

"First off," Liz said, pointedly ignoring Angela, "your test scores were pretty impressive. I'm amazed at some of your answers." She glanced at her desk, strewn with papers. "But none of you got this question."

Angela frowned. "Which one?"

"Fifteen," Liz said. "*Equus* comes from a Greek dialect and it means 'quickness.'"

"No," Angela said. "It means 'horse,' like in equine."

"That's Latin," Robin said. "Aunt Bea asked for Greek."

"What*ever*," Angela drawled. "Who cares about

language?" She examined her fingernails as if they were the most important thing on her mind, and then glanced at Liz. "So, who's on the team?"

Before Liz had a chance to answer, Angela's mother pushed her way into the office. With her was Mrs. James. They wore furtive expressions, like they'd been listening at the door waiting for the right moment to pounce. Kate couldn't be sure, but it looked as if Liz actually flinched.

She said, "As I'm sure you're all aware, I don't pick the team any more, not since my daughter began riding again. The last team was chosen by another trainer; this time I asked Bea Parker to handle it. She's more than qualified, and—"

Mrs. Dean checked her cell phone. "Is this going to take long? I have a committee meeting in ten minutes."

"Not long," Liz said, sounding far nicer than she needed to. She picked up Aunt Bea's clipboard. "Based on all the tests—written, dressage, and jumping—the team for our next event will be Jennifer, Holly, and Kate, with Angela as reserve in case anyone drops out."

There was a ghastly silence.

Kate had never believed people who said, "It was so quiet, you could hear a pin drop," but she believed them now. Even the horses were silent. No sounds of rattling buckets, stomping feet, or anxious whinnies. It was as if something huge had sucked all the air out of the room.

"I won't stand for this," Mrs. Dean said, wagging her bony finger at Liz. "My daughter and Kristina are the best riders here. They absolutely *must* be on this team."

Kate had to look away to keep from laughing. With her dark hair pulled into a bun, her pointed nose, and flowing black cape, Angela's mother could've doubled for the Wicked Witch of the West.

Holly nudged Kate. "Where's Toto?"

"Guarding her broomstick?"

Liz pinned them with a look, then turned to Mrs. Dean. "Bea Parker's decision is final. I'm sure that if Angela works hard, she'll be picked for the next team event." She nodded toward Mrs. James. "And I'm sure that Kristina will, too."

"Come along, girls," Mrs. Dean said, glaring at Liz. "I'll be in touch about this."

"As you wish," Liz said. "But—"

"Save it for later," Mrs. Dean snapped.

In a flurry of indignation, she swept her daughter and Kristina out of Liz's office, followed by Mrs. James who looked slightly uncomfortable. Maybe they didn't have ridiculous scenes like this at Larchwood. According to Adam, it was far less dramatic over there.

For a moment, nobody spoke.

Then Sue thumped Jennifer on the back and Robin gave Holly a shy hug. Liz smiled at Kate and said, "Well done."

"Thanks," Kate said.

Liz's cell phone rang. She listened for a moment and said, "I'll meet you out front."

"What's up?" Holly said.

"Just a hay delivery."

Liz took off, and the girls hung about in her office discussing the horse show. Robin and Sue volunteered to help.

"We'll groom and braid manes," Sue said.

"And we'll clean tack," Robin added. "I'm a whiz at polishing buckles. Even Aunt Bea said so."

"Kristina and Angela will muck stalls," dead-panned Jennifer.

Holly laughed so hard, she almost fell off her chair. But Kate was uneasy. Her joy at making the team was spoiled by the feeling that Angela and her mother had only just begun to make trouble.

8

On Sunday morning, Kate helped her dad with the butterfly museum. This was part of their deal. She would work twelve hours a week in return for him paying Tapestry's room and board at the barn. Everything else—vet bills, farrier, show fees, and new tack—was Kate's responsibility. Luckily, she still had plenty of savings from her summer job and from what she'd earned as a movie stunt double.

The museum was closed until noon, so Kate swept the entrance hall, emptied trash cans, and tidied up from the previous day's visitors. Most had been amateur lepidopterists, anxious to meet the famous Professor Benjamin McGregor, whose books on rare butterflies they could get autographed at the museum's gift shop.

Kate had never seen her father in action before, signing books and talking to his fans like a rock star. Nathan had fans, too, but they weren't nerdy grad students in ill-fitting clothes and horn-rimmed glasses. Nathan's fans were teenage girls who threw themselves at his feet or cut locks from his hair.

Leaning on her broom, Kate tried to imagine her father's fans behaving like Nathan's did. Would they trample one another in their rush to snip bits off his beard and rip the buttons from his tweed jacket? His biggest fan was Mrs. Gordon, the high school principal, who volunteered at the museum on weekends. She also taught biology and had a butterfly collection in her office that even impressed Kate's father.

Someone tapped on the window.

Kate was about to point to the *Closed* sign when she realized it was Brad Piretti. He motioned at her to unlock the front door

"Hi," he said, stepping inside.

He wore faded jeans tucked into his grandfather's brown field boots, and he definitely smelled of the barn. A wisp of hay clung to his collar. He seemed barely able to walk.

"Tough lesson?" Kate said.

"You can say that again," Brad said, groaning.

Sue had been coaching him twice a week and said

he'd almost gotten the hang of posting. Next month, she'd confided to Kate, they would start cantering. "That is," she added, "if Marmalade remembers how."

With another groan, Brad rubbed his thighs. "It's hard work."

"Yup." Kate propped her broom against the reception desk and knocked a pile of baseball caps on the floor. Some were embroidered with butterflies; others had rainbow-colored wings sticking out on each side like Mickey Mouse ears. Kate gathered them up and began to organize them because she had to keep busy, otherwise she'd stare at Brad and embarrass both of them.

He was hard not to stare at.

Sue said that half the girls at school were in love with Brad. Her brother's mossy green eyes and infectious grin had already caused several pileups in the gym. It didn't hurt that he was also the football team's star quarterback. The cheerleaders—led by Angela and Courtney—screamed even louder when Brad Piretti took the field.

"I didn't realize," he said, still rubbing his legs. "I thought you guys just sat in the saddle and let your horses do all the hard work."

"That's what most people think," Kate said. "Some

even complain that equestrian events don't belong in the Olympics."

"Because they look too easy?"

"No," Kate said, "because they're expensive—and elitist."

"So what do they want instead?"

"Shuffleboard and tug-of-war."

"Tug-of-war?" Brad said. "Seriously?"

"Yeah," Kate said, with a grimace. "Even worse than women's beach volleyball."

"Hey, wait up," he said. "I like that one."

"You would," Kate said. "You're a guy."

He shifted from one foot to another. "Is this what you want? To compete in the Olympics?"

"Yes," Kate said. "Most riders do. At least, the ones I hang out with."

There was a pause. "Me, too."

"For riding?" Kate said, astonished.

"Nah, for snowboarding." He gave an apologetic shrug. "I wanna be the next Shawn White."

"Then you'd better dye your hair red," Kate said, and felt herself blush as Brad's eyes swept over her own.

That summer, she'd tried to go blond for her screen test to match the film's glamorous star, Tess O'Donnell.

But it backfired because Tess had to wear a black wig for her *Moonlight* role—and so did Kate. Right now, Kate's hair was half brown and half blond and she couldn't wait for it all to grow out. She grabbed a baseball hat and crammed it over her hateful hair.

"Cute," Brad said, grinning. "Love the butterfly wings."

He had dimples in both cheeks.

Eager to keep him talking about horses, Kate said, "What's the only Olympic sport where men and women compete on equal terms?"

Brad thought for a minute. "Ice dancing?"

"That's done in pairs," Kate said. "Try again."

"How about tennis?"

Kate shook her head. "Nope."

His face cycled through a litany of puzzled expressions, until finally he frowned and put a finger to his lips like a teacher warning his students to be quiet. "Okay, I give up."

"Equestrian," Kate replied. "And it's the only sport with animals involved."

Brad let out a low whistle. "So, who wins? The girls or the boys?" He grinned. "Or the horses?"

"It's pretty even," Kate said, grinning back. "But at the last Olympics, us *girls* swept the medals in dressage."

"The dancing stuff?" Brad said.

Kate sighed and hoped that Sue would eventually straighten him out. "It doesn't take brute strength to get a horse over a jump or to perform a piaffe."

"What does it take, then?"

"Trust, communication, and subtle aids," Kate said, "and some serious bribery with carrots."

"I hate carrots," Brad said.

"Not for you, silly. The horses."

Just then, her cell phone buzzed. Kate checked caller ID and her blush deepened. She loved hearing from Nathan, but why did he always have to call when Brad was around? It was like he had some sort of sixth sense about it.

"I'd better go," Brad said.

Did *he* have a sixth sense as well?

"I guess I'll see you tomorrow," he said, hobbling toward the door. He turned and waved. "At school."

With that, he was gone and Kate discovered she didn't know quite what to say to Nathan whose voice sounded farther away than ever. He'd be home, briefly, for Christmas, he said, in California where his family lived. Then it was back to New Zealand again to finish filming by the end of January. But he had good news.

The *Moonlight* premiere would be in New York

over spring break. The director, Giles Ballantine, was sending tickets to Kate and Holly.

"How many do you want?" Nathan asked.

"Four," Kate said. "No, five." One each for Holly and Liz, Kate and her dad, and Adam.

"Should I send one to Angela?" Nathan said.

"Don't you dare," Kate said.

Like all his other teenage fans, Angela had thrown herself at Nathan when he first appeared on the movie set at Timber Ridge. But he'd ignored her—politely—and made it quite clear that he preferred to be friends with Kate.

Angela was still steaming over that one.

Nathan chuckled. Kate heard snatches of a muffled conversation, something about his teeth and a pancake.

"Breakfast?" she said. It was five a.m. in New Zealand.

"Makeup," he said. "I'm getting fangs."

His character in *Moonlight* was a vampire, but a nice one, Nathan assured Kate. "I only bite the people I don't like."

Kate still hadn't read the book that Holly and her friends raved about. The only good thing about it, as far as Kate could see, was that it had horses in it—even if they did have wings and sparkly hooves. But riding as a stunt double in the film *had* provided Kate with enough money to buy Tapestry and keep her at the barn.

For now, anyway.

Nathan said he had to hang up because the make-up crew couldn't put his fangs in while he was talking on the phone.

"Who was that?" Kate's father said, appearing at her elbow with an armload of books. He glanced at the phone in Kate's hand, then nodded toward Brad's truck, just now pulling out of the parking lot. "Your boyfriend?"

Kate almost said, "Which one?" but caught herself in time. This was ridiculous. She only had one boyfriend.

Nathan Crane.

She'd told her father about him, but he was having a hard time grasping the fact that she was fourteen—almost fifteen—and that boys were now a part of her teenage landscape. Horses, yes. Dad could accept that because they'd always been in Kate's life, but a movie star?

"Brad Piretti," Kate said. "You met him at Holly's party, remember?"

Her father nodded. "Yes, I think so."

"He's just a friend, and his parents run the Timber Ridge ski area." Kate went on. "Brad's an extreme snowboarder."

"*Extreme?*" her father said. "Like all that half-pipe stuff and flipping upside-down?"

"Somersaults and spins," Kate said, laughing. "I haven't seen him do it, but Holly said he's totally rad."

"I'd like to learn," her father said.

"Snowboarding?"

He shuddered. "No, skiing."

"Me too," Kate replied, surprising herself.

"Then we'll have to get your young man to teach us," he said.

Kate bit back a smile. Holly would howl over this. *Young man?* What planet was her father living on?

* * *

An hour later, Kate rode her bike to the barn. The qualifying show was in two weeks and Liz had scheduled team lessons on Sunday afternoons and every day after school. Next Saturday, they were free to ride outside if the weather cooperated, or to practice on their own when the indoor arena wasn't filled with Liz's other students.

Clouds of dust rose from Magician's coat as Holly

groomed him on the crossties. Kate grabbed her grooming box and got to work on Tapestry. She'd been out in the back paddock all night with Magician, and it looked as if they'd had a contest to see which one of them could get the muddiest. Whenever Kate ran over Tapestry's withers with the curry comb, the mare curled her lip.

"You're loving this," Kate said, currying harder.

Next, she used her stiff brush to get out the muck and dirt loosened up by the curry comb, but she could not find her soft body brush to give Tapestry the final touch.

"I've got a spare in my trunk," Holly said. "Use that."

"Thanks." Kate sped off to the tack room.

Holly's battered old trunk lay in the far corner, covered with a pile of summer coolers that needed to be washed. Kate dumped them on the floor and lifted the lid. Its rusty hinges complained.

Bridle parts, frayed lead ropes, and wizened leather riding gloves lay in a tangled heap. Shipping bandages unfurled as Kate pawed through the mess. Beneath two pink rubber bell boots and a set of fleece leg wraps, Kate found Holly's spare body brush. She also found two wooden needles.

For a moment, Kate just stared at them.

What on earth were they doing here? First, it was Angela's ear buds, and now Aunt Bea's knitting needles?

This made no sense at all. It had to be a silly mistake. Aunt Bea must've given the needles to Holly and forgotten all about them.

* * *

At the end of Liz's grueling lesson, Kate was drenched with sweat, but it was more than worth it because Tapestry had performed brilliantly. With a little more leg, she'd dropped her nose and rounded her back. Immediately, Kate sensed the difference. Tapestry's gait was smoother and more comfortable to ride. She actually felt like the dressage horses Kate idolized.

"Good," Liz said. "You used your hands and legs and kept her moving. She's listening to you."

Kate took off her helmet, wiped her brow, and put the helmet back on. Holly rode by and said, "Mom's on a serious roll today. I think I'm going to collapse."

"Me, too," Jennifer said.

With an exaggerated sigh, she threw both arms around Rebel's neck, and Kate caught sight of Jennifer's curb chain bracelet that Holly and Sue had admired the day before. Jennifer said they were all the rage on Etsy.com, so Kate made a mental note to include one on her list of Christmas gifts for Holly.

"What a shame," came Angela's voice.

Holly scowled. "Go away."

Leaning against the arena's double doorway, Angela wore a lime green jacket, white jeans, and platform shoes the color of bubblegum. Her black hair hung loose around her shoulders.

"All that hard work for nothing," she said.

For a moment, she locked eyes with Kate then tossed her head and sashayed back up the aisle, hips swinging like Barbie on a fashion show catwalk.

"Ignore her," Holly said.

Jennifer agreed. "Sour grapes."

They cooled off their horses and led them into the barn. Liz disappeared into the tack room to cope with beginner kids arguing about which ponies they wanted to ride. Parents chimed in, and Kate tuned them out until Holly said, "Mrs. Dean's here."

"Where?"

"She just went into Mom's office," Holly said, "with Angela."

All Kate's anxiety tied itself into a knot and landed in the pit of her stomach. She dumped Tapestry's carrots into her bucket and followed Holly to Liz's office. The door was closed, but Mrs. Dean's voice came through loud and clear.

"Kate McGregor is *not* a resident of Timber Ridge," said Angela's mother. "Therefore, she can't ride in the show."

9

HOLLY GRABBED KATE'S ARM. They'd been through this before when Mrs. Dean tried to block Kate from competing with the team shortly after she arrived at Timber Ridge. It hadn't worked then, and it wasn't going to work now—not if Holly had anything to do with it.

"She's wrong," Holly said.

Pulling away, Kate seemed to shrink into herself. "No," she whispered. "I can't go in."

"Yes, you can," Holly said and yanked open her mother's door. But her confidence took a few steps backward the minute she clapped eyes on Mrs. Dean's triumphant smile. Or maybe it was a sneer. Hard to tell.

Lounging against the wall, Angela wore an expression that matched her mother's. They were like two peas in a very nasty pod.

Holly took a deep breath. "Mom," she said. "What's—?"

"Stay out of this, Holly," her mother replied, sounding weary. "You, too, Kate."

"No," Holly said, still holding onto Kate's arm. "I'm Kate's best friend and I won't—"

Liz held up her hand. "Stop," she said, then turned to Kate. "Mrs. Dean's right. Only residents can ride for the team, and I'm sorry. It's my fault for not paying more attention to the rules."

"But, Mom," Holly protested. "We broke the rules before, when Kate rode Magician in the Hampshire Classic, remember?"

"Yes, Holly," Liz said. "But we didn't break any rules. Kate was a resident then. She lived with us."

"So, she'll just move back in again," Holly said.

Having Kate in her room was like having the sister she'd always wanted. They agonized over boyfriends, argued about favorite horses, and rolled their eyes when parents drove them nuts. They swapped clothes and squabbled loudly, then made up and promised they'd never disagree again—well, not for another five minutes, anyway.

The best thing, of course, would be for Mom to marry Kate's dad. That way, they'd be a complete family. She'd hashed this over with Kate so many times that Holly was almost ready to believe it could actually come true. But as Kate pointed out, this was a fantasy like *The Parent Trap*—Holly's all-time favorite movie.

> *Twins separated at birth reconnect at a teenage summer camp and move several improbable mountains to get their divorced parents back together again.*

Trouble was, Holly and Kate weren't even sisters, let alone twins, and their parents hadn't been married—at least, not to each other.

But Holly refused to give up.

She *would* make it happen—even if she had to sign them both up for an Internet dating service. Now *that* was a cool idea, and it would tie in nicely with Aunt Bea's suggestion about cooking lessons at the high school. Holly's mind began to whirl in a dozen different directions at once.

* * *

Kate caught her breath. Moving back in with Holly and Liz would be the easy way out, but it was a lot more complicated than that. She'd just begun to form a real relationship with her father. They were muddling along in Aunt Marion's cottage and actually making a go of it.

Kate's mom would've been proud. She'd always been the bridge between Kate and her father, but after she died, the connection almost fizzled out because Dad was always gone. Now he was home for good, and Kate was afraid of messing up what they'd started to build together.

Angela shattered Kate's reverie.

"Don't worry, Kate," she said, sounding sweeter than a box of chocolates. "You can still be part of our team. I need a groom, and I hear you do wonderful braids."

Holly exploded.

Eyes flashing like a fireworks display, she turned on Angela. "You're a phony. You ride for the ribbons, not because you care about horses."

"That's not important," said Mrs. Dean. "My daughter is a star, and she's on the team."

Angela smirked. "See?"

There was an awkward silence, then Liz said, "Okay, Angela. We'll see you at team practice tomorrow after school."

Miserably, Kate exchanged looks with Holly, but they both knew Liz meant business. She'd been out maneuvered, and there was nothing she could do about it.

"I'm sorry, Kate," Liz said, after Angela and her mother departed. "I can't change the rules. I wish I could, but—"

"I understand," Kate said, close to tears.

But inside, she was seething. Despite Angela's never-ending sabotage, Kate had helped the Timber Ridge team win blue ribbons all summer. Sadly, the only blue ribbons that counted with Mrs. Dean were those that Angela won. Nobody else's mattered.

The show would go on without Kate.

Her mother used to say, "Trying your best and feeling good about yourself is more important than winning ribbons."

Wiping her eyes, Kate missed her mom more than ever. So, instead of riding, she would honor her mother's memory by grooming for Holly and Jennifer. She would cheer them on, but she would not cheer for Angela.

"I'm sorry," Holly whispered.

In a small voice, Kate said, "No big deal."

But it was.

Without being part of a recognized riding team, Kate had no chance of competing in the Festival where she just might be noticed by the USET talent scouts—one of her biggest dreams.

She'd have to find another way to get there.

* * *

Angela wasted no time telling everyone at school about being on the Timber Ridge team. She made it sound as if they didn't have a hope of winning without her.

"Way to go," said one of the cheerleaders.

Another squealed and waved her pompoms. Hulking boys in cleats and shoulder pads hoisted Angela into their arms and carried her around the gym like a trophy. It seemed as if the entire football team was impressed by her news.

Except for Brad.

He shot Kate a sympathetic look and hobbled off, still walking carefully because he'd just had another riding lesson with his sister. Kate decided that was kind of cool—about the only cool thing that had happened in the past three days. Even Holly, who'd gotten all caught up in team practice, had forgotten how bummed out Kate was feeling.

Jennifer was also bummed out.

Her curb chain bracelet had gone missing. They'd turned the barn upside down looking for it, but no luck. Jennifer said she'd get another, but it wouldn't be the same because hers had been unique—a one-off made by a jewelry artist who'd gone on to other things.

Holly said, "Maybe you'll find a better one."

"With horse charms," Sue suggested.

Jennifer gave her a withering look.

* * *

"What's wrong?" Kate's father said.

Kate shrugged. "Nothing."

They'd just finished work at the butterfly museum and were back in Aunt Marion's kitchen sharing a pizza. It was Kate's favorite—sausage with extra cheese—yet she could only manage half a slice.

"You're not eating," he said.

Kate pushed her plate away. "I'm not hungry."

There was a pause while her father cut two more slices, slid one onto her plate, and pushed it back toward her. "It's about the team thing, isn't it?"

"Yeah," she said, surprised that he'd figured it out.

She hadn't said a word, but maybe Liz had told him. Kate couldn't bring herself to talk about it, not even to Holly. It hurt too much.

He said, "Is there another team you could join?"

"I guess so," Kate said, "except I don't want to."

Just thinking about it made her feel like a traitor. She couldn't imagine riding for Larchwood, Spruce Hill Farm, or Fox Meadow Hunt Club. They were Timber Ridge's biggest rivals. Holly called all of them the enemy—well, except for Adam, of course.

"Why not?" her father said.

"Because they cost a fortune," Kate said.

But that wasn't the only reason. Mostly, it was about loyalty. Her father wouldn't understand. He'd recently lost his position at a university he'd devoted his life to and then been kicked out without so much as a cheap watch to mark the twenty years he'd put in. Right now, loyalty to jobs and teams wasn't high on his list of priorities.

"Like, how much?" he said.

She hesitated. "Five hundred." That's what it cost at Larchwood, but Adam's parents paid only half that amount because Adam paid off the rest by working at the barn.

Kate's father took a bite of pizza and got cheese on his beard. She handed him a napkin. "Isn't there any other way?" he said.

The words were out before Kate could stop them. "You and Liz could—" She clapped a hand over her mouth.

Get married.

"Could what?" he said.

Backtracking madly, Kate said, "Liz could help us find a house at Timber Ridge."

"Kate," he said, gently. "You know we can't afford it. Not right now, anyway."

"But we've got to move in the spring," Kate reminded him. "Aunt Marion will be home, and she'll need her cottage."

He sighed. "I know, and I'm working on it, okay?"

Aunt Marion's black cat, Persy, leaped onto Kate's lap and began making dough. His sharp little claws dug through her jeans and into her legs like miniature needles.

Needles?

In all the riding team trauma, she'd forgotten to ask Holly about them.

* * *

With Kate calling out instructions, Holly worked on her dressage routine. It was based on a first-level test, but the riders were encouraged to throw in a few more complicated movements as well. Then they had to memorize them.

Magician was brilliant at that.

When Kate rode him at the Hampshire Classic last spring, she was so nervous she'd forgotten which way to turn after riding down the centerline, but he remembered.

"Keep it simple," Holly's mother said, over and over. "Figure out what your horse does best and go with that."

Angela refused to listen.

"I'm going to do a pirouette," she said, holding up her arms like a ballerina.

"In a tutu?" Jennifer said.

Sue laughed so hard, she tripped over a traffic cone and landed face down in the tanbark. Liz told her to pull herself together or leave the arena, but Holly could see that her mother was struggling not to smile.

But not Mrs. Dean.

Her face was a mask of fury as she sat in the observation room. The only reason she didn't come flying out to interfere was because she couldn't walk across the arena in her stupid high heels. Instead, she crouched there like a spider, watching and taking notes. Yesterday she'd had a meltdown because Mom had criticized Angela for having a dirty bridle.

"Did Kristina forget to clean it?" Kate muttered.

She was being a good sport about not being on the team, but Holly knew how much it hurt. For two years, she'd sat in a wheelchair and watched other girls—including Kate—ride Magician and win the blue ribbons she used to win. Even now, looking down at her legs, Holly found it hard to believe she was actually in the saddle again.

Mom's voice got her attention.

"Come on, girls, stop dreaming. We've got work to do. The show's tomorrow, so let's get busy."

10

THUNDERING HOOVES WOKE KATE before dawn. For a moment, she didn't know where she was. Above her head, wild horses galloped across the ceiling. Had *they* woken her up?

Of course not, stupid.

It was Holly's miserable alarm clock.

Kate reached out and thumped the snooze button. The noise stopped. Yawning, she glanced at her best friend, still asleep in the other bed.

"Wake up," Kate said, barely awake herself.

Another minute ticked over. It was now five o'clock. They had to be on the road by seven, which gave them two hours to get dressed, groom Magician, and braid his mane. Holly had wanted to do it the night before, but Kate disagreed.

"He'll lie down and get all messy," she said. "Or he'll rub his neck and pull the braids out."

"Okay, then *you* get up early and do it," Holly retorted. "I'll sleep for an extra hour."

Kate scrambled out of bed. She tried to rip off Holly's comforter and they ended up in a tug-of-war. But it did the trick. Holly woke up and claimed first dibs on the bathroom—just like old times.

After scarfing down orange juice and bagels, they packed their knapsacks and headed for the barn. Robin, Sue, and Jennifer were already there. So was Brad. With a confident grin, he picked up a bale of hay like it weighed no more than a pillow and threw it over one shoulder. Kate half expected him to snip the baling twine with his teeth.

"Show-off," Sue said.

He bent to pick up another, but Liz stopped him. "Just dump this one in the horse van, okay?"

"Sure," Brad said. "Then what?"

His sister handed him a broom. "Sweep out the feed room. It's a mess."

Brad shrugged. "Okay."

"Wow," Holly said. "You're well-trained."

"Housebroken," said Robin.

"More like barn-broken," said Jennifer, from the depths of Rebel's stall.

Everyone had shown up except Angela.

She'd probably arrive at the last minute—or not at all—and expect someone else to have groomed her horse. Skywalker paced his stall, back and forth like a pendulum. Angela had given him a half-hearted brushing the night before and covered him with a cooler. She hadn't even bothered to clean her tack.

Gently, Brad punched Kate's arm with his broom handle. "Wanna come and help me?"

"Yeah, okay," she said, without thinking.

Holly gave her a sharp nudge. "Magician's mane?"

"Oh," Kate said. "Sorry. I can't."

"No problem," Brad said, and trundled off with the hay.

Holly dragged Kate into the tack room. She pulled elastics and a mane comb from her grooming box and thrust them at Kate. "What's up with you guys?"

"Who?"

"Don't play dumb," Holly said. "You and Brad."

Kate stared at her. "There is no *Brad and me*. He's just a friend."

"Oh, yeah?" Holly said. "Brad's a snowboarder, so why is he hanging out at our barn all the time?"

"Because he likes horses?"

Holly snorted. "Does Nathan know about this?"

"No, but Brad knows all about Nathan," Kate said.

"So stop imagining things, okay?" Dumping her knapsack on a chair, Kate raced back to Magician's stall. She was already confused enough. She didn't need Holly to make things any more complicated than they already were. If someone had written the rules about dating boys, Kate hadn't read them. She had no idea what to do. Brad was just a friend, wasn't he?

Magician nuzzled her hand.

Kate wrapped her arms around his warm neck and remembered the first time she'd braided his mane for a show. Angela had tried to mess that one up as well.

"Move over," Holly said, sliding into place beside Kate. "My turn."

After giving him an extravagant hug, Holly buffed Magician's ebony coat with a body brush while Kate separated his mane into small bunches. She braided them tightly, folded them under twice, and secured each one with an elastic. By the time she was done, Kate's fingers were sore and Magician had fifteen knobby little braids along the crest of his neck.

Leaving Holly to finish up her horse, Kate slipped into the adjoining stall to give Tapestry her fair share of hugs. She and Magician were best friends, just like Kate and Holly. The two horses hated being separated, even for a few minutes. If Angela hadn't ruined everything, Kate would be grooming Tapestry the way she'd just groomed Magician. She'd have braided Tapestry's mane into tiny little topknots and polished her hooves, and—

The barn door banged open, and Angela sauntered down the aisle. Behind her came Kristina, carrying Angela's hunt jacket, her helmet, and a yellow sports bag. Kristina shot Kate a scornful look as she walked by.

"Bratface," Holly muttered.

"Bratface number two," Kate corrected.

"No, three," Holly said. "We forgot Courtney."

But she hardly counted these days. Now that Kristina was Angela's new groupie, there was no need for Courtney. At least, not around the barn. Angela's cousin was probably relieved. She'd always made it quite clear how much she hated the place.

Ten minutes later, Liz told the girls to load up their horses. Robin and Sue carried out armloads of equipment—buckets, grain, and grooming boxes—and Brad shoved another bale of hay into the storage compartment. Liz added emergency flares, jumper cables, and first-aid supplies. Angela complained that she needed more time to groom Skywalker.

Liz tapped her watch. "You should've gotten here earlier."

Still grumbling, Angela led her horse outside and, as

usual, had trouble getting him on the van. After much coaxing, he finally followed Rebel up the ramp and Liz secured both horses in side-by-side compartments. A fine layer of sweat covered Skywalker's mahogany shoulders. He flattened his ears and kicked at the partition that separated him from Jennifer's horse.

To Kate's surprise, Magician balked as well. He trod on Holly's foot and almost knocked her over. Patiently, she waited until he calmed down and tried again. She tempted him with a carrot. Magician put one hoof on the ramp, whinnied, and backed off. From the barn, came an answering whinny.

"What's up with him?" Liz said, clearly in no mood for another stubborn horse.

Holly patted his neck. "He wants Tapestry."

"How about I load her first?" Kate said. "He'll follow her in, and once he's on board, I'll take her out." She really didn't want to do this because it would upset Tapestry as well, but if it would get Magician on the van, then—

"Magician will go ballistic," Holly said.

"So let's bring Tapestry with us," Liz said, checking her watch again. "We don't have time to mess about."

"But she's a disaster," Kate wailed. "I haven't braided her mane or—"

"Who cares?" Angela snapped. "You're not in the show."

Kate flinched. Angela was right, but it hurt anyway. With Holly close behind, she ran back into the barn and stuffed Tapestry into a halter, then helped Holly wrap her legs with fleece pads and shipping bandages.

"Get your saddle," Holly said. "And your bridle."

"Why?"

"Duh-uh," Holly said, rolling her eyes. "So we can ride together between my classes."

Kate shrugged. "Okay."

It wasn't the same as competing, but it would be better than not riding at all. While Holly led Tapestry outside, Kate raced down the aisle. She shot into the tack room and bumped straight into Kristina James.

"You forgot this," she said, holding out Kate's knapsack.

* * *

"I don't trust her," Holly said. "I bet she took something."

They were in the van's back seat. Brad sat up front beside Liz. She'd put him in charge of the GPS, and he was taking it seriously, convinced he could find a better route to Fox Meadow Hunt Club by punching in different coordinates. Sue and Robin had gone with Jennifer and her parents. Bringing up the rear were Angela and Kristina in Mrs. Dean's luxurious Mercedes.

Kate rummaged through her knapsack's main compartment. Her water bottle, wallet, and cell phone were all there, along with fleece mittens and an extra sweatshirt. She checked the front pocket, and her fingers brushed against something hard and cold.

Frowning, Kate pulled it out.

Holly gasped. "That's Jennifer's bracelet."

They stared at the curb chain dangling from Kate's fingers. Then a dozen light bulbs went off in Kate's head. "She's trying to frame us."

"Who?" Holly said.

"Kristina James," Kate said, thinking fast. "She must've taken Angela's ear buds and left them on your bridle peg, and I think she stole Aunt Bea's knitting needles as well."

"Needles?" Holly said. "What needles?"

"The ones Aunt Bea said had gone missing," Kate said. "I found them in your tack trunk."

"Why didn't you tell me?"

"Because I figured Aunt Bea had given them to you and then forgotten she'd done it." Kate shifted in her seat. "And then I kind of forgot about it, too."

She looked out the window. A gray landscape

rushed past—barren fields and bare trees. The only splash of color was an occasional red barn or a white church steeple.

Holly sighed. "Okay, we know Kristina's a bratface, but why is she taking stuff and making it look as if we're doing it?"

"Because she likes causing trouble?"

"That's obvious," Holly said. "But I think it's more than that." She wrinkled her nose as if she'd just smelled something bad. "I bet you anything that Princess Angela dared Kristina to do it. Kind of like an initiation sort of thing. You know, the stuff some kids at school make you do before they'll let you into their stupid little clique."

Kate had never been invited to join a clique, so she didn't know how it all worked. Quietly, she said, "Or maybe Kristina just wants to stir up trouble between you and me."

There was a stunned silence, and Kate could almost hear Holly's brain ticking over, just the way hers was. Then Holly caught her breath. "You didn't think *I'd* taken that stuff, did you?"

"No," Kate said, trying not to feel guilty.

But that's exactly what she'd thought. Holly had been super mad at Angela for messing up her party and when Holly got mad, well, almost anything could happen. She'd once pushed Angela into the swimming pool after Angela told one of Holly's friends she was too fat to wear a bathing suit.

"You did," Holly said. "You really thought *I'd* stolen Angela's ear buds and Aunt Bea's needles, didn't you?"

Miserably, Kate nodded.

"Don't feel bad," Holly said, looking chagrined. "If I'd found Jen's bracelet in your knapsack, I'd have—"

"Assumed I'd taken it?" Kate said.

"Yeah," Holly said. "So that makes us even."

Kate gave her a fist bump. "I'm sorry."

"Me, too," Holly said. "So, has Kristina planted stolen goods on anyone else?"

"Not as far as I know," Kate said. "But even if she had, wouldn't they have said something about it?"

"Sue would," Holly said.

Kate nodded. "So would Jennifer."

"So what're you going to tell her?"

Kate hadn't thought that far ahead. "The truth, I guess."

"Let's think about it first," Holly said. "We don't want to start a barn war. Not today, anyway. We've all got to pull together."

The van lurched around a corner. Kate's knapsack

when flying, and she grabbed the armrest to keep herself from toppling into Holly.

"We're almost there," Brad announced.

Leaning forward, Kate stared out the front window. Nestled amid rolling hills, Fox Meadow Hunt Club was an impressive complex of horse barns, indoor arenas, and well-groomed fields bordered by crisp, white fencing. According to Liz, this event attracted teams from all over Maine, Vermont, and New Hampshire.

Lines of trucks, vans, and SUVs filled one large paddock. In another, riders warmed up their horses. Someone fat and jolly, dressed in a Santa suit, was handing out lollipops. Beside him stood a fuzzy brown Shetland with reindeer horns and a bright red ball attached to its halter.

"Rudolph, the red-nosed pony," Holly said.

Kate grinned. In all the trauma about the show, she'd completely forgotten that Christmas was less than two weeks away.

Besides, it wasn't even cold enough. The weather forecast called for temps in the forties today.

A woman with a clipboard checked off Liz's name and waved her toward a parking space behind a gooseneck trailer. Two rows over was the Larchwood van.

Grooms bustled about, unloading horses and equipment.

"There's Adam," Holly said, pointing.

She yanked open the door and leaped out. But before she'd even taken a step, Kristina James emerged from the back seat of Mrs. Dean's car and got to him first.

"Adam," she gushed. "It's so cool to see you."

Then, she kissed him.

11

Holly clenched her fists. She wanted to claw Kristina's smug face with every fingernail she possessed. Blinded by anger, she raised a hand, ready to strike.

Someone grabbed her arm.

"Don't," Kate said, dragging her away. "She's doing it on purpose, to get at you. It's part of their plan. Don't you see?"

Holly couldn't see anything right now except Kristina James trying to steal her boyfriend. Her fingers itched to score a hit on Kristina's perfectly smooth cheeks.

"Calm down," Kate said, once they were out of earshot. "Think about it. Angela knows she can't beat you, so she's set Kristina up to rattle your cage. She wants to make you so mad that you won't be able to ride properly."

"So why is she making Kristina do it?" Holly said, jerking free of Kate's grasp. "Why not piss me off herself? She's been doing it ever since kindergarten."

"She's a bully," Kate said. "And she's a coward. Ignore her."

But Holly couldn't.

She'd been Angela's victim long before Kate arrived at Timber Ridge. In the early days, Holly was the rising star. While Angela goofed off, Holly had trained hard. She rode in all weathers, she mucked stalls till she dropped, and she brought home the trophies and blue ribbons that Mom needed to keep her job as the barn's winning trainer. If the riding team didn't win, Mrs. Dean threatened to replace Mom with somebody else.

Then came the car accident, and Holly wound up in a wheelchair. Angela pretended to be sympathetic, but inside she was gloating. Finally, *she* would be the golden girl.

For two years, it worked.

With Mrs. Dean's influence and a new push-button horse, Angela won every prize on the junior circuit—until Kate McGregor showed up and Holly's legs started working again.

"Let's hustle, girls," her mother said.

Swallowing hard, Holly came back to earth with a bump. She helped Kate and Jennifer unload horses while Brad and Sue unloaded equipment. At Liz's request, Robin raced off to collect their numbers and a program from the show tent. Angela failed to show up, so Holly unloaded Skywalker as well. The sweat on his neck had dried into crusty little swirls as if he'd been smothered in whipped egg whites.

"This'll impress the judges," Holly muttered to herself, as she began to brush Magician. It would serve Angela right if she totally blew it, just like she did last year.

Mrs. Dean had crawled all over her for not qualifying, but Holly had a suspicion that Angela didn't really care. Oh, she loved the glory of winning ribbons, but she also loved jerking her mother's chain. It probably explained why Angela rode like a dream on some days and like a sack of potatoes on others.

"Heads up!" someone yelled.

A loose horse came thundering by. Reins flapping, it swerved to avoid a couple of Jack Russell terriers and bumped hard into Magician's hindquarters.

"Oh, no," Holly cried as her horse stumbled.

Immediately, Kate dropped to her knees. She ran her hands up and down Magician's hind legs, then stopped at his left fetlock.

"He's hurt," she said, glancing at Holly.

"Where?"

"Pastern," Kate said. "Look."

A tiny bead of blood seeped out of a small cut, just enough to stain the circle of hair above Magician's hoof. The blood trickled down and made Holly's heart skip a beat. It might be nothing, or—

Her mother said, "Walk him, and let's see."

Holly crossed her fingers, but Magician favored his leg and limped along like a three-legged dog. Unable to stop herself, Holly burst into tears. It was almost as if Angela had engineered this one, too.

* * *

Liz cleaned the wound, covered it with a sterile dressing, and pulled an ice pack from the cooler. Holly held it against Magician's pastern, tears streaming down her face.

"He'll be okay, won't he?" Kate said.

"Yes," Liz replied, standing up. "It's just a surface cut, and he'll need a tetanus booster, but I'm afraid Holly can't ride him today."

So what would that do to the team's chances? Did they need three riders to compete, or could they manage with only two? Kate hadn't checked the rules because she wasn't riding. She didn't think Holly had checked them either.

As if reading her mind, Liz said, "I'd better talk to the show committee. We might not be able to compete with only—"

Tapestry nudged Kate so hard, she almost fell over.

"She wants a carrot," Holly said.

Liz gave a wry smile. "She wants attention."

Another light bulb went off in Kate's head. "No," she said, handing Tapestry's lead rope to Holly. "She wants to compete . . . with *you*."

Holly stared at her. "Are you serious?"

"Yes," Kate said.

Voices faded, horses quieted down, and background noises disappeared. For a few precious moments, it was just Kate and Holly caught in a bubble only they could understand. Their eyes met and something indefinable, but very special, passed between them. It was almost like a relay race where one runner hands off the baton to the next runner and trusts her to do get the job done.

Kate trusted Holly.

She'd only ridden Tapestry a few times, but Kate also trusted her mare to perform. Tapestry wouldn't let either of them down.

Wide-eyed, Holly turned to her mother. "Can I ride Tapestry? I mean, would it be okay?"

"I don't see why not," Liz said, consulting her notes. "When I filled out the entry form, I only wrote down the riders' names, not the horses'." She looked at Kate. "Are you sure about this?"

"Yes," Kate said.

She knew, without a doubt, that Holly would do the same for her. In fact, she already had. Stuck in a wheelchair, Holly had convinced her mother to let Kate to ride Magician in the Hampshire Classic. She hadn't complained about it either. Kate wanted to hug her.

Holly was the best friend ever.

After Liz got Magician settled in the van with a hay net and plenty of water, Robin ran up with a program and their show numbers. Liz handed them out. Kate clipped the plastic disc with number 193 to Tapestry's bridle and ran her fingers over the V-shaped browband that Holly had given her. It had a line of tiny fake pearls across the middle, just like the ones they'd admired on the latest Olympic dressage horses. Kate wasn't too sure about the bling, but Holly loved it.

* * *

Liz got the show committee to rearrange its schedule so that Holly would ride last. This gave her more time to school Tapestry and jump a few practice fences.

She rode into the outdoor ring beside Adam. He'd managed to shed himself of Kristina James and appeared to be totally focused on Holly. They were competing for the same prizes, but it didn't seem to matter. They laughed and joked with each other like Kristina had never even happened.

Kate wanted to take notes.

She wanted to learn more about this whole dating thing that Holly knew far better than she did. Looking at Holly now, you'd never know that half an hour ago she'd been ready to thump Adam for letting Kristina kiss him.

Behind them, Angela thundered up on Skywalker. Angela held him so tight with her double reins that Skywalker's head dropped behind the vertical.

"*Rollkur*," Sue whispered.

Kate nodded. She'd seen videos of it, and she'd learned the Wikipedia definition by heart: *"flexion of the horse's neck achieved through aggressive force."*

That's what Angela's old trainer had taught her, but he'd been fired. Unfortunately, Angela hadn't forgotten his extreme methods. She was forcing Skywalker to bend his nose so far inward that it almost touched his shoulders.

* * *

Riding Tapestry was totally different from riding Magician. Holly adjusted her seat and her hands, and allowed herself to flow into the mare's gentle rhythm. As Kate called out the dressage test movements that Holly had memorized with Magician, she discovered that Tapestry had memorized them as well.

How did that happen?

Had the two horses swapped notes in the barn?

Trying not to giggle, Holly swung Kate's mare into a collected trot. Tapestry's ears flicked back and forth like antennae, waiting for Holly's next signal. Two smooth strides, and they were cantering along the rail. Then, back to a walk, followed by another canter, complete with a spectacular flying change across the diagonal.

Wow, Holly thought. *This is amazing.*

"Sweet," Adam said.

Putting her reins in one hand, Holly blew him a kiss with the other. She edged Tapestry closer to Domino, but Angela got in the way. Breathing hard, Skywalker pounded between them. Gobs of foam flew from his mouth and stuck to his shoulders. Veins erupted along his neck like miniature mole tracks. If Angela kept this up, Skywalker would be ready to explode by the time they reached the dressage ring.

Liz called her riders together for last-minute instructions. "They've split us into two groups," she said, sliding up the keepers on Rebel's bridle. "We're in Group A which means we'll be doing dressage in Arena One this morning, and jumping in Arena Two this afternoon. Group B does the opposite."

Holly glanced at Adam.

The Larchwood trainer was having the same conversation with his riders. They were in Group B, which meant that Holly and Adam might have a chance to watch each other's rides.

"When will they judge our tack?" Holly said.

Kate had cleaned Tapestry's saddle and bridle the night before, not realizing how important it would turn out to be. And as soon as Holly had finished practicing a few jumps with Tapestry, Kate would braid her mane as well. Sue had volunteered to help.

"Shortly before your dressage test," her mother said. "So make sure it's nice and clean."

"What about the ribbons?" Angela said.

Liz sighed. "There aren't any. This show is all about

qualifying. It's a pass–fail situation. You'll get a certificate if you qualify, but no ribbons. Those come at the Festival in April."

Angela pouted. "They had ribbons last year."

"How would you know?" Holly muttered. "You didn't win any."

Angela didn't appear to have heard, or if she did, she ignored it. Yanking off her helmet, she tossed her head and rode off with Kristina trotting beside her like an obedient puppy.

* * *

Liz took over helping Holly with Tapestry. She said the mare would probably do better without Kate breathing down her neck and suggested that Kate might like to check out the two indoor arenas.

Brad asked if he could tag along.

"Yeah, sure," Kate said, not feeling the least bit sure.

Was this like a mini-date? Would Brad want to hold her hand and try to put his arm around her? They'd slow-danced at Holly's party, but that was different. Kate shoved both hands firmly in her pocket.

The arenas were huge, but Kate had never seen one as enormous as the Fox Meadow jumping arena. It had skylights, flying buttresses, and bleachers that rose to the ceiling. At the far end stood a pavilion filled with important looking people—judges, show officials, and special guests. A couple of them wore red Santa hats.

Brad whistled. "It's bigger than a football field."

"You ought to know," Kate said.

She scanned the massive arena. This was a combination show jumping/cross-country event, so the course designer had mixed brightly painted oxers with rustic crossrails, logs, and a fake stone wall. To Kate's relief, there was no sign of a chicken coop. For Tapestry, this was almost perfect, except for—

"Uh-oh," Kate said.

"What?" Brad said.

Kate pointed. "The Liverpool."

"Huh?"

"A water jump," Kate said. It was half hidden behind a large Christmas tree surrounded by tubs of red poinsettias. Even worse, it was the third jump and had a very short approach.

"So, do you jump it or paddle in it?" Brad said.

"Sometimes you swim in it," Kate said, taking a closer look. She'd seen Liverpools that got riders tossed off and had them doing the backstroke. But this one was small—a kids' wading pool tucked beneath a red-and-green oxer. Tapestry had never jumped one before.

Horses were unpredictable.

It was hard to tell what would set them off. Last week, while riding down the road toward Jennifer's house, Tapestry had freaked out over a baby carriage. But five minutes later, when a motorcycle roared past, she didn't even bat an eyelash.

Liz said it was all about noise.

For some odd reason, horses coped with stuff that made a noise but totally lost their marbles over bicycles and squirrels and scraps of paper that made no noise at all. Who knew what would happen when Tapestry met the Liverpool?

12

JENNIFER NAILED HER DRESSAGE TEST. Rebel arched his neck and wowed the audience with a perfect extended trot. Then it was Angela's turn, and Skywalker acted like a total spaz. He fought the bit and skittered sideways until Angela lost her temper and whacked him with her crop.

"Not good," Liz muttered.

Kate gulped. Angela's rotten performance wasn't Liz's fault. It was because Angela never showed up for team practice. But Mrs. Dean wouldn't see it that way. At any moment, she'd swoop down from her privileged seat in the judge's pavilion and pick Liz apart like a vulture. Then she'd probably tear Angela to pieces, but in private.

Holly ran up. "We've got a problem."

"Angela?" Kate said.

"No," Holly replied. "Tapestry's browband. I can't find it."

An hour ago, Kate and Sue had braided Tapestry's mane while Holly took her bridle apart to give it another cleaning. Browbands were important. They kept the headstall from creeping forward over a horse's ears and falling off.

"Where did you leave it?" Kate said.

Holly waved toward her grooming box, sitting on the van's side ramp. Two brushes and a curry comb had fallen out. "I ran to the bathroom and when I got back, the browband was gone."

"Then we'll have to use Magician's," Kate said. "It's the same size."

But that wasn't the point.

They both loved that special browband. Holly had originally bought it for Magician at the same auction where they'd found Tapestry, but she'd decided it didn't work on Magician, so she'd given it to Kate as a "welcome to the barn" gift for her new horse. Since then, Tapestry had worn it for every show and special event, and it had become something of a talisman, like the horseshoe charm that Robin always carried in her pocket and Sue's faded blue ratcatcher she refused to compete without.

"Kristina," Holly sputtered. "I bet it was her."

"Looks like it," Kate said.

Angela and Kristina had been in and out of the van all morning. Either one of them could easily have taken that browband. Would Holly's stirrups disappear next or her helmet?

"I'm gonna tell Mom," Holly said.

"No," Kate said. "She's got enough to deal with. Mrs. Dean's going to shred her over Angela's dressage ride."

Holly snorted. "That wasn't a ride. It was a—"

"Bad joke?" Kate said.

She helped Holly reassemble Tapestry's bridle with Magician's browband and noticed that Holly's number, 193, added up to thirteen. Kate wasn't superstitious, but just to be sure, she decided to avoid ladders and black cats. The Fox Meadow barn was probably full of them—along with Jack Russell terriers, and they'd already caused enough trouble.

* * *

Moments before Holly entered the arena, Kate whipped out her cloth and wiped the dust off Holly's boots. Aunt Bea had texted earlier to wish them both good luck. She had no idea that Kate wasn't on the team. They'd decided not to tell her, at least not till it was all over.

"I'm scared," Holly whispered. "Suppose I mess up?"

"You won't," Kate said, with more confidence than she felt. It wasn't easy, performing a dressage test on a horse you'd only ridden a few times.

Nobody would know Holly was nervous because she looked the part. She wore a navy hunt jacket and pale pink ratcatcher—birthday gifts from Liz—and the gloves Kate had given her. Even Holly's show breeches had come clean in the wash, thanks to a little hand scrubbing to get the grass stains out of the knees.

The judge's bell rang.

Holly adjusted her helmet and trotted into the arena. The bleachers were only half full, which was probably a good thing. In the front row, Jennifer sat with Sue and Robin. Behind them, Adam and Brad gave Holly a combined thumbs up. Adam wore a big grin. He'd just a scored a clear round in his jumping class, along with a big hug from Holly.

Liz said, "Thanks for letting her ride Tapestry."

"No problem," Kate said.

It was kind of weird and wonderful, all at the same time, watching her horse perform. She'd seen Holly ride Tapestry on the trails at Timber Ridge when they swapped horses, but never like this—in front of an audience with the barn's reputation at stake.

Halting at X, Holly saluted the judges.

Tapestry's copper-colored coat gleamed brighter than a newly minted penny. Her tail shone like spun gold, and fifteen button braids carved an elegant scallop down her neck. At the letter C, Holly turned right and began to float through the dressage test's alphabet soup as if she'd ridden Tapestry all her life.

Kate could hardly believe it.

It was like riding the mare herself. She could feel what Holly felt. Her legs sensed that moment when a working trot transitioned into an extended trot. She cantered through a flawless flying change with Holly and wanted to shout with glee. Then came a shoulder-in that was so perfect Kate's mouth dropped open.

This was fourth-level stuff.

"Well done," said the Fox Meadow trainer, patting Liz on the back.

Holly grinned from ear to ear as she rode from the arena to a standing ovation. She flung her arms around Tapestry's neck and dropped a dozen kisses on her mane, just the way she always did with Magician.

Angela snorted. "Cheat."

Her mother bustled up and waved the show's regulations beneath Liz's nose. "This isn't right. You're not allowed to switch horses."

"Sorry," Liz said. "But we're okay with this one."

Kate wondered how Mrs. Dean was going to justify her daughter's abysmal dressage test. But maybe, just maybe, Angela would redeem herself with a brilliant jumping performance.

It had happened before.

Angela was famous for pulling startled rabbits out of unlikely hats.

* * *

They got an hour's lunch break. Kate locked Holly's tack in the van's storage compartment and pocketed the key. She didn't think Angela and Kristina would be dumb enough to do any more damage, but it was best to play it safe.

At the Hampshire Classic, Angela had pulled a string of dirty tricks to beat Kate for the individual gold medal. She'd messed up Magician's stall right before the judges came by and moved markers on the cross-country course so that Kate would get lost. And finally, when Kate didn't think anything else could possibly go wrong, her stirrup flew off when she was halfway through her show jumping class.

Holly had wanted to confront Angela, but Kate wouldn't let her. They had no proof, and besides, Timber Ridge won the challenge trophy despite

Angela's attempts at sabotage. She didn't care about the team; all she wanted was the gold medal.

The food tent was crammed solid. After grabbing burgers, fries, and soft drinks, Kate and Holly squeezed into a picnic bench with Brad, Adam, and Jennifer. The rest of the team sat with Liz, except for Angela who was cruising the crowd like a tabloid photographer, snapping pictures with her cell phone. She took several of her mother, sitting at the head table with show officials and judges, then took one of Santa, still handing out lollipops.

"I guess he's not a dentist," Brad said.

"Smile for the camera," Angela said, appearing out of nowhere. She shot a photo of Holly and Adam, then aimed her cell phone at Brad and Kate.

"Go away," Jennifer said.

Ignoring her, Angela checked her phone. "Sweet," she said, and waved it toward Kate.

She caught a glimpse of herself, looking wide-eyed beside Brad. His arm was draped around her shoulders. When did that happen? Feeling awkward, she scooted further up the bench.

"Too late," Angela said, and sauntered off.

"What was that all about?" Brad said.

Adam took a slug of his soda. "I dunno."

But Kate did. She had a nasty feeling that Angela would post her renegade photo on Nathan's Facebook page. Not that it mattered. His fan page was managed by the studio's PR department, and Nathan never looked at it.

Nudging her, Holly whispered, "Who's that woman?"

"Where?" Kate said.

"Sitting next to Mrs. Dean."

Kate almost did a double take. The woman was about twenty-five with white-blond hair and a pretty smile, and she was whippet thin, like a jockey. If Kate didn't know better, she'd have guessed this was Ineke Van Klees. But what would a world-famous dressage rider be doing at a junior horse show in Vermont?

* * *

Magician was behaving like a wing nut. As long as Tapestry was in the van with him, he was perfectly calm, but the minute she left, he thrashed about like a fish in a bucket. Holly brought him outside and let him graze on a lunge line. He was still limping, but not as badly as before.

"I'm going to take him home," Liz said.

"How?" Holly said.

"Fox Meadow has loaned me a truck and trailer so

I can leave the van here," her mother replied. "I'll get back as soon as I can."

Robin offered to go with her.

"Thanks," Liz said. "That would be great."

"I'll hang out at the barn if you like," Robin said. "Maybe Magician could go out in the paddock with Daisy. She was his girlfriend before Tapestry, remember?"

They double wrapped his legs with fleece and coaxed him onto the Fox Meadow trailer with the last of their carrots. Holly could hear his whinnies till the truck was almost out of sight. The minute it disappeared, she felt guilty. She ought to have gone with Magician, but Mom needed her team to do well. Angela had pretty much blown it, so it was now up to Jennifer and Holly.

And Tapestry.

They had two hours, maybe more, until their turn to jump. The butterflies in Holly's stomach were already doing cartwheels. By the time they got into the ring, they'd probably be looping the loop like an aerobatics team. She didn't get this nervous with Magician because she knew him so well, but Tapestry was unknown territory. She'd gone over the practice fences fine, and she'd carried Holly through a brilliant dressage routine, but—

"C'mon," Kate said, grabbing her hand. "Stop day-dreaming. Adam's up next."

* * *

Kate and Holly found seats with Jennifer, Sue, and Brad. While Adam warmed up in the collecting ring, Kate glanced around the arena. That blond woman was in the judge's pavilion, sitting beside Mrs. Dean. From the looks of it, Mrs. Dean was giving her an earful.

"Who *is* that?" Kate said, trying not to be obvious about pointing.

Jennifer said, "Don't you recognize her?"

"Yeah," Kate said. "She looks like Ineke Van Klees, but—"

"That's because she *is*."

Kate felt herself gawping like a goldfish. *Ineke Van Klees?* Her all-time favorite dressage star? She rode for the Dutch equestrian team and won her first Olympic medal at nineteen. Kate idolized her the way other girls idolized rock stars.

So how did Jennifer know it was her?

Kate was about to ask when it hit her. Of course, Jennifer knew Ineke Van Klees. She'd trained under Jennifer's grandmother, Caroline West, at Beaumont Park, one of England's most prestigious equestrian centers. Mrs. West had invited Kate and Holly to spend part of next summer there with Jennifer. They would get to work with riders like Nicole Hoffman and Will Hunter, two more of Kate's favorite superstars.

"Is she—?" Kate faltered. "Is she, like, one of the dressage judges?"

"No," Jennifer said. "She's here looking at some horses to buy for my grandmother, and—"

"Hush," Holly said. "Adam's in the ring."

Kate tried to concentrate on Adam's test, but it went by in a blur. All she could think about was meeting Ineke Van Klees. Jennifer had promised to introduce her. What would she say? Would she act all goofy and tongue-tied, the way teenage girls acted around Nathan?

There was a round of applause.

Holly hooted and whistled, so Kate figured that Adam had done well. He jumped off his horse, and Holly flung her arms around him. They were still hugging one another when Kate slipped out of the arena with Jennifer to help her get ready for jumping.

* * *

Jennifer and Rebel had a clear round, followed by Angela, who pulled the proverbial rabbit out of its hat with a stunning performance that brought Mrs. Dean to her feet. Skywalker sailed over the jump course as if the fences were no bigger than shoe boxes. His hind foot tipped the hogsback, but it didn't fall, and he didn't even hesitate at the Liverpool.

Mrs. Dean couldn't stop talking about it.

She carried on like an infomercial to anyone who'd listen, gushing about her incredible daughter and how she'd be the next Olympic star. But when Kate overheard Angela crying in the ladies' room ten minutes later, she knew that Mrs. Dean had slammed into her about the dressage test.

Muffled sobs came from the end stall.

As quietly as possible, Kate washed her hands in the bathroom's shallow sink and was about to leave when the door swung open and Angela slouched out, sniffling and wiping her eyes.

She stared at Kate. "What are *you* doing here?"

"Using the bathroom?" Kate said.

"Ha ha, very funny," Angela snapped. Pushing Kate to one side, she twisted the faucet so hard that water spurted out and splashed all over her. "Now look what you made me do."

Kate handed her a paper towel. "I'm sorry."

And she was, not because of Angela's wet breeches, but because of her vile, two-faced mother. No wonder Angela was a brat. Mrs. Dean was either praising her to the max or threatening to ground her for life. Kate couldn't begin to imagine what it was like to have a mother like that. Her own had been the complete opposite. She'd loved and encouraged Kate until the day she died.

A tear escaped.

"Don't cry for me," Angela said.

Kate sucked in her breath. "I'm not."

The bathroom door banged open, and Kristina barged in. She shot a scornful look at Kate, and whatever sympathy Kate had felt for Angela disappeared like water down the drain.

13

ANXIOUSLY, HOLLY KEPT A LOOKOUT for her mother. She was supposed to be here by now.

Was Magician okay? Holly wondered. Did he survive the ride home without making his leg any worse?

Holly checked her cell phone but Mom hadn't texted or left a message. Even Kate wasn't around. She'd gone to the bathroom ages ago and hadn't come back. Maybe she'd gotten sick. Those hamburgers they ate in the food tent were kind of gross.

Holly's stomach churned but she knew it wasn't from the burgers. She was scared stiff about jumping Tapestry. Their dressage test had gone fine, but what if they totally messed up in the big arena? Tapestry was cool, but she wasn't reliable like Magician. Sometimes she freaked out over stupid stuff, like chicken coops and baby carriages.

Kate had warned her about the Liverpool.

That summer, they'd taken Tapestry to the lake. Kate had no clue how her new horse would react to water, but she loved it. She got down and rolled the way Magician always did, splashing like a wild thing. But Rebel, who refused to go anywhere near water, had jumped the Liverpool without a qualm.

So had Skywalker.

It was hard to predict what a horse would do one way or the other, so Holly crossed her fingers and tacked up Kate's mare. Tapestry pricked her ears, as if she were tuned into Holly's thoughts.

"Girl power," Holly said, tidying up Tapestry's braids. "We're not gonna let two wimpy geldings outjump us, okay?"

Tapestry whickered, which meant only one thing—she'd spotted Kate.

"Where have you been?" Holly said, as Kate ran up.

"Bathroom," Kate said. "Angela was having a meltdown."

"Why?" Holly said. "Skywalker had a clear round."

Kate shrugged. "I think Mrs. Dean slammed into her for that dressage test."

"Better than her slamming into Mom," Holly said.

"Is she back yet?"

"No." Holly tightened Tapestry's girth. "I'm worried about Magician. Suppose his leg is worse and Mom had to call the vet."

"Then she'd have also called you," Kate said. "So stop worrying." She looked around. "Did my browband show up?"

"Nope," Holly said. "I'll get you another. I'm going to the auction next Saturday with Adam. He wants to buy his mother riding gloves for Christmas, like the ones you got for me."

She pulled them on, and the soft, buttery leather felt like a whisper against her fingers.

* * *

Kate couldn't deny it. She was envious of Holly riding Tapestry over jumps that she ought to be riding her over. They weren't huge, and Tapestry had jumped ones just like them before, except for that unexpected Liverpool.

A chicken coop would've been better. Tapestry hated coops, but she'd learned to jump them, despite being terrified of chickens.

When Kate first saw Tapestry, trapped in a field owned by a scary old hermit, his scruffy roosters had been kings of the heap. They pecked at anything that moved. Ever since then, Tapestry had been wary of critters with feathers, and Kate had spent hours—and countless carrots—convincing her mare that jumps disguised as chicken coops were nothing to be afraid of.

"She's gonna balk at the Liverpool," Kate said, as they headed for the outside practice ring. "So keep her moving and focused. Don't let her run out. Give her a flick with your crop if you need to."

The loudspeaker blared, calling out the final batch of numbers. Holly's was at the tail end, and Kate wished for the millionth time they were competing together instead of—

Angela stalked past.

Her face was a blank mask—no sign of her crying jag in the bathroom. She stared right through Kate like it never happened. Beside her, Kristina led Skywalker, covered with dry sweat. It was almost as if he'd been crying as well.

* * *

The course map was a maze of arrows and dotted green lines. Holly counted nine jumps, including a tricky combination. Quickly, she memorized the twists and turns and hoped that Tapestry wouldn't bring it all to a gigantic halt by stopping for a snack at the hay-bale jump or freaking out over the Liverpool. This wasn't a timed event. You just had to get through the course with as few faults as possible.

Jennifer had gone clear. So had Angela.

Holly caught her breath. She had to go clear as well and then hope for the best. Mom said that more teams were competing tomorrow, and they wouldn't get the results until Monday. Out of almost two hundred riders, only the top twenty from this show would qualify for the Festival of Horses next April.

A Larchwood rider left the ring. She'd knocked down two jumps and run out at another. The next rider was from Spruce Hill Farm. Holly recognized him, Derek something-or-other. He'd flirted with Courtney at the hunter pace and told her the correct time which had allowed Angela to cheat.

Holly wanted him to fail. Badly.

And he did.

His bay mare trashed the crossrails, demolished the brush jump, and stopped dead in front of the Liverpool. Derek went flying over her head and landed in the kiddie pool. A few giggles erupted from the bleachers. Angry and soaking wet, Derek got back on his horse and finished the course, but he certainly wasn't going to qualify with a round like that.

Kate looked at Holly. "Are you okay?"

"Yeah," Holly said, as the ring steward signaled her to enter the ring. Her stomach clenched and unclenched like a fist. Her hands sweated inside the leather gloves. Tapestry pricked her ears, as if she knew something important was about to happen.

Kate patted her neck. "Don't let me down."

"She won't," Holly said, scanning the crowd. Still no sign of Mom.

From Tapestry's back, the jumps looked larger than they did from the ground. Did she remember the course? Holly wracked her brain, but her mind had gone fuzzy. *First, the crossrail, then the brush, but after that . . . what? Turn left and jump the Liverpool or straight ahead to the double oxer?*

To give herself more time, Holly circled twice, trying to clear her head, but as she approached the first jump, it all clicked into place. Over the crossrail they went, then the brush, and Holly swung a hard left toward the Liverpool. She leaned so close to Tapestry's mane, the braids tickled her nose.

"It's only water," she said. "Don't be scared."

Tapestry hesitated. Her ears swiveled like antennae

as if to say, *I'm not sure about this*. But thanks to Kate, Holly was prepared. She clamped her legs against Tapestry's sides, and they catapulted forward. Up and over the Liverpool they went, clearing it by more than a foot.

Tightening her left rein, Holly curved toward the hogsback. It had three red-and-white rails, the middle one higher than the other two. On each side were full-size cutouts of reindeers. It was like jumping Santa's sleigh. Just before they took off, Holly caught sight of her mother standing with Kate.

Holly felt herself relax.

She cantered a right-hand loop around the stone wall and aimed for the logs. They looked solid, like a real cross-country jump, but Holly knew they weren't. They fell apart if a horse touched them. The run-up was long, so Holly slowed down a little. There was no rush. Tapestry's ears swiveled back and forth. That was a good sign; she obviously didn't think this was a chicken coop. Holly moved into a half-seat.

One, two, three . . .

Tapestry flew over the logs and landed square. Next up, the combination. But as they approached the stack of hay bales, Holly could feel Tapestry falter. Two horses had already stopped dead at this delicious jump and made the crowd laugh by eating it.

"This is *not* a snack," Holly warned.

From the judge's pavilion came a deep voice. "That's telling her."

Holly grinned and pushed Tapestry forward. Over the hay bales they went, two big strides, then over the green-and-white parallel bars. The minute they landed, Holly pulled Tapestry into a hard right to face the double oxer. No big deal, except for the window box full of poinsettias that sat beneath it.

Weren't those poisonous? Holly couldn't remember.

Flanking the jump were fake Christmas trees festooned with tinsel and red bows. Brightly colored gift boxes lay in heaps around each tree. The course designer had gone a little overboard with this one. Leaning forward, Holly felt Tapestry gather herself up. She rocked back on her haunches, tucked her front legs, and—

Clang!

"Aahhhh," went the audience.

Holly held her breath. She heard the rail wobbling in its metal cups and cringed as she waited for the inevitable thud that would slam her with four faults. She didn't even dare look behind in case it threw Tapestry off her stride.

"Oohhhh," breathed the crowd.

The rail held and Holly sighed with relief.

One more jump to go—the stone wall. It looked like a real one, but Holly knew the stones were fake—just like the logs—and wouldn't hurt if a horse banged into them. Several already had, and the ring stewards had a fine old time putting them back together again.

Sizzling with energy, Tapestry bounded toward it.

Holly held her in check until the last minute, then let her go. Over the wall they soared, and for a moment, Holly felt as if she were flying. Up and up. Would they ever come back to earth? She'd once read a book where an Olympic horse crash-landed at the last jump and broke both its front legs.

Thud!

Tapestry's feet hit the ground and she kept on going, past the finish post. They were home free, with a clear round, and, best of all, safe.

* * *

Tapestry arched her neck as they cantered out of the ring. Kate whooped and hollered. Mom's smile was so big it almost jumped off her face. Holly felt herself being pulled from the saddle. Someone, probably Kate, threw a blanket over Tapestry. Sue began to lead her away to cool off.

"Wait up," Holly yelled.

She wrapped her arms around Tapestry's sweaty neck. "I love you," she cried. "You're amazing."

"She's the best," Kate said.

More arms joined the hug fest. Adam lifted Holly off her feet and swung her around. Brad just stood there, grinning like he'd had something to do with it all. Jennifer gave Holly a high five.

"Way to go, dude," she said.

Once they disentangled themselves, Kate replaced Tapestry's bridle with a halter and fed her a carrot. The mare crunched it down, noisily and messily. Smears of pale orange horse slobber landed on Holly's white breeches.

"Hey," Holly said, wiping it off. "I thought we used up all the carrots with Magician."

Magician!

She'd forgotten all about him. "Mom, how's—?"

"Doing fine," Liz said, holding up her phone. "Robin just called. He's out in the back paddock with Daisy, and he's not limping anymore."

"That's because he's too busy chatting up his old girlfriend," Sue said.

Kate grinned. "Tapestry's gonna be *so* jealous."

Everything—relief, tension, and joy—jammed themselves into such a big, overwhelming lump, that Holly threw herself into her mother's arms.

Liz staggered backward. "Hey."

"Thanks, Mom, for everything," Holly said, fighting tears. She'd cried more in the last few hours than she'd cried since her father died. He'd have been so proud of her. He didn't know one end of a horse from the other, but he'd mucked stalls, attended every show, and—

"When do we get the results?" said a voice behind her.

Holly stiffened and pulled away. Trust Mrs. Dean to ruin a family moment.

14

LEADING TAPESTRY BACK TO THE VAN, Kate wondered how Liz managed to put up with Mrs. Dean. She'd demanded to have the final results, like *right now*, but no matter how many times Liz explained the show's rules, Angela's mother refused to listen.

"I know the judges," she'd said.

Liz put on her most patient smile. "So talk to them."

"I will," said Mrs. Dean and stalked off.

But it didn't do any good. The show officials merely repeated what Liz had said. The results wouldn't be available on their web site until Monday afternoon. Not that it mattered. Angela's dressage disaster had cooked her chances of qualifying.

Holly wasn't too sure.

"I bet you anything Mrs. Dean bribes the judges. She tried last year, and it almost worked, but—"

"You can't be serious," Kate said.

"Dead serious," Holly replied.

Kate argued that she'd heard of people gaming the system, but surely Fox Meadow was above all that. They were one of the biggest show barns in Vermont. Would they risk their reputation just to appease Mrs. Dean and her spoiled brat of a daughter?

"Money talks," Holly said, rubbing her fingers together like Scrooge. She held Tapestry's halter while Kate wrapped the mare's legs with fleece pads and shipping wraps. "Just remember that Mrs. Dean is richer than Donald Trump."

A gross exaggeration, but Kate got the point.

She gave a little shiver—partly from being creeped out, but mostly because the weather had gotten colder. Kate zipped up her vest, then loaded Tapestry onto the van. In the adjacent stall, Jennifer adjusted Rebel's hay net.

"Do you still want to meet Ineke?"

"Yes," Kate said. "Where is she?"

"Right here," said a voice Kate didn't recognize. There was hardly a trace of an accent.

The Dutch superstar gave Kate a dazzling smile.

Feeling like a klutz, Kate smiled back and hoped she didn't have spinach on her teeth.

Spinach?

She hadn't eaten spinach since last week's pizza pig-out with Holly, and that was because of Liz. She'd insisted that their pizza have at least some sort of green vegetable on it.

"Jennifer tells me this is your horse," Ineke said.

Kate gulped. "Yes."

With a well manicured hand, Ineke Van Klees patted Tapestry's neck and Kate decided she would never brush her mare again.

Oh boy, how dumb was that?

She was acting worse than Nathan's spazzed-out fans. One of them, according to his Facebook page, had given up washing her hair because it had brushed against Nathan's shoulder.

"She is Morgan, yes?" Ineke said.

Wordlessly, Kate nodded.

"They are good dressage horses," Ineke said. "Tomorrow, I go to see a Mr. North in New York. He breeds Morgans, and—"

It all came out in a rush.

Kate spoke so fast, that Ineke asked her to slow down. Finally, Kate forgot how nervous she was and explained the connection between her and Richard North and Tapestry.

"Why do you not ride her yourself?" Ineke said.

Kate exchanged looks with Jennifer.

There was no point in trying to explain how Mrs. Dean had manipulated the riding team's residency rules to keep Kate from competing. Ineke wouldn't understand. Or maybe she would. Kate had heard that the world of international riding was pretty cut-throat.

To Kate's relief, Jennifer changed the subject. "I'm going to England next summer, to ride with my grand-mother. Kate and Holly are coming with me."

"This is good, very good," Ineke said. "You will learn all about eventing and have a good time."

Holly yelled up the ramp. "Mom's ready to leave."

Angela had left Skywalker, still sweaty, tied to the van, so they loaded him as well. Kate threw a blanket over his back. She didn't want him getting a chill on the ride home. Brad hopped into the cab with Holly, and Kate was about to follow when she noticed something on the ground.

Tapestry's browband?

It was muddy and kind of bent like it had gotten trampled or run over by a car. Some of the little pearls had gone missing. Maybe it had been there all along, and they'd overlooked it.

Maybe Kristina hadn't taken it after all.

* * *

Jennifer's parents had left earlier, so Jennifer rode in the van's back seat with Kate and Holly. Sue was up front sitting between her brother and Liz. Brad wanted to try a different route, but Liz overruled him.

Kate shot a glance at Holly. They'd already agreed to ignore their suspicions over Kristina's odd behavior. They had no proof she was behind the missing items. If they accused her, it could all come crashing around their ears. Mrs. Dean would get involved, and Kate wanted to avoid that at all costs. Slowly, she pulled Jennifer's bracelet from her knapsack.

"Where did you find it?" Jennifer exclaimed.

"In Liz's lost-and-found bucket," Kate said, following the script she'd rehearsed with Holly.

It was totally believable.

Liz was always plucking odds and ends off the barn floor—buttons, braiding elastics, broken spurs—and tossing them into a bucket in her office where she promptly forgot about them. She could've easily mistaken Jennifer's bracelet for an ordinary curb chain.

"I was looking for my hoof pick," Holly said, "and I found your bracelet instead."

Kate glanced at Jennifer and hoped she wouldn't ask why they hadn't told her right away. But she didn't. With a grateful smile, Jennifer clipped the chain around her wrist and held it up.

"Thanks, guys. I owe you."

They were halfway home when the sky darkened and it began to snow—big fat flakes that stuck to the road and the van's windshield. Kate was trying not to admire the way Brad's hair curled over his collar when he turned around.

"Skiing tomorrow," he said with an infectious grin that could stop a stampede. "Who wants to come with me?"

* * *

On Sunday morning, Kate rushed through her chores at the museum. She swept the floor, tidied the gift shop, and made sure her father's books were well-displayed. Mrs. Gordon was using one of them for her biology classes and had encouraged teachers in other school systems to do the same. Dad was beyond thrilled.

"Maybe I'll write a novel next," he said, "about a teenager who loves butterflies, and he—"

"Make him a *zombie* teenager who loves butterflies, and you're golden," Kate said, pulling a silly face.

For a moment, it looked as if he was about to take her seriously. Dad's sense of humor wasn't always on the same wavelength as hers.

At lunchtime, he drove her home and listened to music in the car while she changed into warmer clothes—long underwear, multiple layers of fleece, and the snow pants she'd borrowed from Holly. On her way out the back door, Kate grabbed her down parka and stuffed herself into that as well. She climbed back into her father's car feeling like the Pillsbury doughboy.

"All set?" he said, switching off the radio.

Kate nodded. "Yeah, I think so."

But inside, her heart was thumping like sneakers in a dryer, and her thoughts ran wild. Was she completely nuts, letting Brad Piretti teach her to ski? Suppose she fell and broke her arm or her leg? What then? She wouldn't be able to ride or help Dad. She'd be useless around the barn.

But skiing was just as risky as riding a horse, and so far she'd not broken any bones. Well, except for her little toe when Webster, her first pony, trod on it.

* * *

After two hours on the bunny hill, Kate could not believe how much her thighs burned, to say nothing of her knees. Even her fingernails hurt. As she struggled to follow Brad down the gentle slope, Kate decided she would never, ever tease him again about being sore after his riding lessons.

Skiing and riding demanded different leg muscles.

So did ballet.

When Kate's mother was a little girl, she took ballet and riding lessons. Then she met a famous ballerina who'd also loved horses as a kid. The ballerina explained that in ballet you turned your legs and feet outward; with riding you kept them pointing forward. This developed different leg muscles, and the ballerina said she had to make a choice: breeches or tutus.

To this list, Kate added ski boots.

They forced her legs into such an unnatural position that she wanted to scream. Finally, after she learned to snowplow and not fall every time she got off the chairlift, Brad declared she'd had enough for one day. They retreated to the lodge where a log fire burned and hot chocolate arrived in large mugs with lots of whipped cream on top.

Brad said, "Did you have fun?"

"Kind of," Kate said, rubbing her legs.

He grinned. "Touché."

It took a moment to register, then Kate laughed. Feeling like she'd been mangled by a snowblower, she understood exactly how Brad had felt after his first riding lesson.

"Payback?" she said.

"No," Brad said. "I just thought you'd enjoy learning to ski."

And she had. Sue and Robin clumped into the lodge, followed by Jennifer. Shucking off their ski boots, they parked themselves on benches in front of the fire. The only person missing was Holly, but she was on a date with Adam. They'd gone Christmas shopping at the mall.

Mentally, Kate checked off the gifts she'd bought—a curb-chain bracelet for Holly, two books on dressage for Liz, multicolored sock yarn for Aunt Bea, and sheepskin slippers for Dad. The only thing left was to print up a gift certificate for the cooking lessons she and Holly had bought for their parents.

But what about Nathan?

Mailing a package to New Zealand would cost more than the gift itself. Besides, it was far too late to send anything now. And would Brad give her a gift, which meant she'd have to give him one as well?

This whole boyfriend thing was a big muddle. Holly skated through it like an Olympic ice dancer. She had one guy. Kate appeared to have two, and she had no idea what to do about it.

"We're going out for pizza," Brad said. "Wanna come?"

15

On Monday, Kate kept a close eye on Nathan's fan page. She peeked at her cell phone when teachers weren't watching, checked it obsessively at lunch, and spent last period study hall in the computer lab.

So far, Angela hadn't posted her photo.

Nathan had texted early that morning. Kate agonized over telling him about Brad, but what was there to tell? They'd gone skiing together, shared a pizza, and hung out at the barn. Oh yes, they'd danced kind of close at Holly's party . . . and at Halloween.

Big deal, right?

Not compared to Nathan's antics in New Zealand —that is, if you believed the gossip mags. Their latest rumors had Nathan jetting off to Hawaii with Tess O'Donnell for Christmas. The two stars would be exchanging gifts over a candlelight dinner on the beach.

Romantic Getaway, screamed one headline.

Another shouted, *Is It Time for a Ring?*

Holly told Kate to ignore them. She reminded Kate that Nathan was seventeen and so was Tess. They both had college plans. Whatever the stupid magazines said, they were all lies.

To distract herself, Kate pulled up the barn's Facebook page and looked at photos of Tapestry instead. Liz had gotten a fabulous shot of her in midstride, extending across the arena. The dapples on her rump glowed like a checkerboard; her tail glistened as if sprinkled with fairy dust. For a few magical moments, Kate imagined the feel of her reins, that subtle contact with Tapestry's mouth, and—

Holly raced into the lab. "Are they up yet?"

"What?" Kate said.

"Duh." Holly grabbed another chair and launched the Fox Meadow web site. It took a few moments to load, and by the time it did, Holly had turned pale and closed her eyes.

"You look," she said. "I can't."

Kate didn't want to look either, but one of them had to. She scrolled down the list. It was alphabetical, by team, and Holly's name appeared first, followed by Jennifer's. But not Angela's.

"Your party," Kate said.

Holly opened one eye. "What?"

"You wanted to pay her back, right?" Kate said, savoring the moment. It was fun, spinning out the suspense. Holly did it to her all the time.

"Yeah," Holly said. "But what does—?"

"'The best revenge is massive success,'" Kate said, quoting one of Holly's favorite movie stars. The only reason she knew about it was because her English teacher was a bigger film buff than Holly. She was always coming out with trivia like that.

"Frank Sinatra?" Holly said.

"Yup."

"So?" Holly said.

"So you've beaten Angela, you dummy," Kate said. "She's not on the list." Not that Kate expected her to be, despite what Holly said about Mrs. Dean bribing the judges. There was no way Angela was going to qualify, not after that dressage fiasco.

"Wow!" Holly said. "Are you sure?"

Kate laughed. "See for yourself."

She zoomed in on Holly's name so that it showed up larger than a headline. For a moment, Holly just stared at it. "Did Jennifer make it?"

"Yes," Kate said. "So did Adam."

"Whoopee!" Holly cried. She leaped out of her chair so fast it shot backward and crashed into a couple of kids who were sharing a computer in the next cubicle.

* * *

The high school was three blocks from Aunt Marion's cottage. They burst through the back door, giggling and still whooping with glee. Holly hadn't been there since the day after Kate and her dad had moved in when it had been full of unpacked boxes, suitcases, and towering piles of books.

"Nice," she said, looking around Kate's tiny bedroom on the second floor. It was almost a mirror image of her own. Horse posters covered the walls, show ribbons framed a corkboard, and Kate's barn clothes lay strewn across the floor. Completing the familiar picture was Holly's pony print comforter on Kate's unmade bed. In the middle of it, Persy was nonchalantly washing his paws.

Holly plunked herself down beside him. Purring like a toy motor boat, he climbed onto her lap. She stroked his coal black fur and wished they could get a cat, but Mom was allergic. She sneezed whenever the feral barn cats came near. Good thing she wasn't allergic to horses as well. That would really stink.

Persy dug his claws into her thighs.

"Ouch," Holly said. Maybe a cat wasn't such a good idea.

After Kate had finished changing, they walked back to school and caught a late bus to the barn. Holly's mom was in the arena with a bunch of beginner kids.

Had she seen the show results?

Holly checked the laptop in Mom's office, but the last web site she'd visited was her favorite online tack shop, and that had been at noon. Kate said the results hadn't come out until two-thirty.

Holly grabbed her grooming box from the tack room, and by the time she reached Magician's stall, Kate already had him in the crossties. She was crouched down, feeling his pastern.

"Was he limping?" Holly said. Because of the snow, he'd been cooped up in the barn for two days and might have gotten stiff.

"Nope," Kate said. "I think he's fine. What did the vet say?"

"No riding for a week," Holly said.

"Then we'll share Tapestry." Kate fed Magician a carrot and gave another to Tapestry.

Holly grinned. "Or I could ride Plug."

He was all of twelve hands, and she'd ridden him during her therapeutic riding lessons while still in her wheelchair. It had marked the beginning of her recovery. She loved that little brown pony, even if he was as stubborn as a stone.

The barn door slid open, and Angela cruised toward them. Behind her came the ever-faithful Kristina James. Holly still couldn't understand why a girl like Kristina kow-towed to a bully like Angela, especially when Kristina was something of a bully herself.

Angela said, "Where's Liz?"

"Giving lessons," Holly replied.

"I need to see her," Angela said, folding her arms. She wore riding boots and breeches and a yellow hoodie with *Rolex Kentucky* embroidered on the front. "Like, right now."

"Is it about the results?" Holly said.

Angela shrugged. "Those don't matter," she said and headed for the indoor arena.

Holly yelled after her. "I mean it, Angela. Mom's busy. She's got lessons all afternoon."

Angela stopped so abruptly, Kristina bumped into her. She whirled around, hair flying in all directions. From his stall, Skywalker gave an anxious whinny. Then Cody neighed, and in less than two seconds, the other horses joined in. Magician jerked his head and snorted.

"Too bad," Angela said, "because *I* need a lesson."

"Why?" Holly said, immediately suspicious. Angela had never bothered with riding lessons before and insisted she didn't need them.

"Because I'm competing in the next show," Angela said. "As an *individual.*"

This stopped Holly dead in her tracks.

Individual?

The qualifying shows were all about teams. You had to be on a team in order to compete. Had they suddenly changed the rules? Had Mrs. Dean stuck her nose into this and caused a major fuss?

"What are you talking about?" Kate said.

Angela gave a sly smile. "That's for me to know and you to find out."

Holly's mind zoomed into overdrive. If the rules *had* changed, they'd changed in the last twenty-four hours, and she doubted that Mom had seen them. But, if Angela was right and individuals could compete, this meant that Kate—

She glanced at Kate and realized she was thinking the same thing. They gave each other a mental fist bump.

But Angela picked up their vibes. "Don't even think about it," she said. "Kate isn't allowed to ride."

"Why not?" Holly said.

"Because the rules say that two different riders can't ride the same horse, and *you* already rode Tapestry." Angela paused, as if for dramatic effect. "Which means Kate can't ride her in the next show."

There was a stunned silence.

Holly shot a look at Kate, then draped her arm over Magician's rump. "In that case," she said, enjoying every word, "Kate will ride my horse instead.

Don't miss **TAKING CHANCES, Book 7**
in the exciting **Timber Ridge Riders** series,
coming in October, 2013

About the Author

MAGGIE DANA'S FIRST RIDING LESSON, at the age of five, was less than wonderful. She hated it so much, she didn't try again for another three years. But all it took was the right horse and the right instructor and she was hooked.

After that, Maggie begged for her own pony and was lucky enough to get one. Smoky was a black New Forest pony who loved to eat vanilla pudding and drink tea, and he became her constant companion. Maggie even rode him to school one day and tethered him to the bicycle rack ... but not for long because all the other kids wanted pony rides, much to their teachers' dismay.

Maggie and Smoky competed in Pony Club trials and won several ribbons. But mostly, they had fun—trail riding and hanging out with other horse-crazy girls. At horse camp, Maggie and her teammates spent one night sleeping in the barn, except they didn't get much sleep because the horses snored. The next morning, everyone was tired and cranky, especially when told to jump without stirrups.

Born and raised in England, Maggie now makes her home on the Connecticut shoreline. When not mucking stalls or grooming shaggy ponies, Maggie enjoys spending time with her family and writing the next book in her TIMBER RIDGE RIDERS series.